They Never Get Caught

Ruskin Bond is known for his signature simplistic and witty writing style. He is the author of several bestselling short stories, novellas, collections, essays and children's books; and has contributed a number of poems and articles to various magazines and anthologies. At the age of twenty-three, he won the prestigious John Llewellyn Rhys Prize for his first novel, *The Room on the Roof*. He was also the recipient of the Padma Shri in 1999, Lifetime Achievement Award by the Delhi Government in 2012, and the Padma Bhushan in 2014.

Born in 1934, Ruskin Bond grew up in Jamnagar, Shimla, New Delhi and Dehradun. Apart from three years in the UK, he has spent all his life in India, and now lives in Landour, Mussoorie, with his adopted family.

They Never Get Caught

Edited and compiled by
RUSKIN BOND

RUPA

Published by
Rupa Publications India Pvt. Ltd 2021
161-B/4, Gulmohar House,
Yusuf Sarai Community Centre,
New Delhi 110049

Sales centres:
Bengaluru Chennai
Hyderabad Kolkata Mumbai

P-ISBN: 978-93-90918-79-9
E-ISBN: 978-93-90918-87-4

Eighth impression 2026

10 9 8

Printed in India

CONTENTS

INTRODUCTION

It is late in the night as I write this introduction to a new horror collection. It's also a very cold night up here in the mountains. And I think, if I'm not mistaken, snow has started to fall outside. It makes for the perfect setting for some good old horror classics.

Over the years, I have written several horror stories and edited compilations on the genre. And if you have enjoyed shuddering your way through my earlier volumes of scary stories, then you will find satisfaction in this spooky sequel too. With a repertoire of ghostly themes, claustrophobic setting, and threatening situations, the grisly tales in this volume will not disappoint young horror addicts. From empty houses, ghostly dolls and laughing skulls to haunted villages, shapeshifting jackals and vengeful cats—prepare to encounter dangerous elements and explore uncharted territories created by some of the masters of the genre.

So, watch your step and look around. These hair-raising stories are guaranteed to make your flesh creep. I think this book will make for a perfect read on long winter evenings of drawn curtains and dim lights; or summer nights with the moon streaming in at the window and perhaps a jackal howling not very far away. Foxes dancing in the moonlight will be more beautiful than scary, but they will be around too.

Ruskin Bond

THE PHANTOM COACH

Amelia B. Edwards

The circumstances I am about to relate to you have truth to recommend them. They happened to myself, and my recollection of them is as vivid as if they had taken place only yesterday. Twenty years, however, have gone by since that night. During those twenty years I have told the story to but one other person. I tell it now with a reluctance which I find it difficult to overcome. All I entreat, meanwhile, is that you will abstain from forcing your own conclusions upon me. I want nothing explained away. I desire no arguments. My mind on this subject is quite made up and, having the testimony of my own senses to rely upon, I prefer to abide by it.

Well! It was just twenty years ago, and within a day or two of the end of the grouse season. I had been out all day with my gun, and had had no sport to speak of. The wind was due east; the month, December; the place, a bleak wide moor in the far north of England. And I had lost my way. It was not a pleasant place in which to lose one's way, with the first feathery flakes of a coming snowstorm just fluttering down upon the heather, and the leaden evening closing in all around. I shaded my eyes with my hand, and staled anxiously into the gathering darkness, where the purple moorland melted into a range of low hills, some ten or twelve miles distant. Not the faintest smoke-wreath, not the tiniest cultivated patch, or fence, or sheep-track, met my eyes in any direction. There was nothing for it but to walk on, and take my chance of finding what shelter I could, by the way. So I shouldered my gun again, and pushed wearily forward; for I had been on foot since an hour after daybreak, and had eaten nothing since breakfast.

Meanwhile, the snow began to come down with ominous steadiness, and the wind fell. After this, the cold became more intense, and the night came rapidly up. As for me, my prospects darkened with the darkening sky, and my heart grew heavy as I thought how my young wife was already watching for me through the window of our little inn parlour, and thought of all the suffering in store for her throughout this weary night. We had been married four months, and, having spent our autumn in the Highlands, were now lodging in a remote little village situated just on the verge of the great English moorlands. We were very much in love and, of course, very happy. This morning, when we parted, she had implored me to return before dusk, and I had promised her that I would. What would I not have given to have kept my word!

Even now, weary as I was, I felt that with a supper, an hour's rest, and a guide, I might still get back to her before midnight, if only guide and shelter could be found.

And all this time, the snow fell and the night thickened. I stopped and shouted every now and then, but my shouts seemed only to make the silence deeper. Then a vague sense of uneasiness came upon me, and I began to remember stories of travellers who had walked on and on in the falling snow until, wearied out, they were fain to lie down and sleep their lives away. Would it be possible, I asked myself, to keep on thus through all the long dark night? Would there not come a time when my limbs must fail, and my resolution give way? When I, too, must sleep the sleep of death. Death! I shuddered. How hard to die just now, when life lay all so bright before me! How hard for my darling, whose whole loving heart but that thought was not to be borne! To banish it, I shouted again, louder and longer, and then listened eagerly. Was my shout answered, or did I only fancy that I heard a far-off cry? I halloed again, and again the echo followed. Then a wavering speck of light came suddenly out of the dark, shifting, disappearing, growing momentarily nearer and brighter. Running towards it at full speed, I found myself, to my great joy, face to face with an old man and a lantern.

'Thank God!' was the exclamation that burst involuntarily from my lips.

Blinking and frowning, he lifted his lantern and peered into my face.

'What for?' growled he, sulkily.

'Well—for you. I began to fear I should be lost in the snow.'

'Eh, then, folks do get cast away hereabouts fra' time to time, an' what's to hinder you from bein' cast away likewise, if the Lord's so minded?'

'If the Lord is so minded that you and I shall be lost together, friend, we must submit,' I replied; 'but I don't mean to be lost without you. How far am I now from Dwolding?'

'A gude twenty mile, more or less.'

'And the nearest village?'

'The nearest village is Wyke, an' that's twelve mile t'other side.'

'Where do you live, then?'

'Out yonder,' said he, with a vague jerk of the lantern.

'You're going home, I presume?'

'Maybe I am.'

'Then I'm going with you.'

The old man shook his head, and rubbed his nose reflectively with the handle of the lantern.

'It ain't o' no use,' growled he. 'He 'ont let you in—not he.'

'We'll see about that,' I replied, briskly. 'Who is he?'

'The master.'

'Who is the master?'

'That's nowt to you,' was the unceremonious reply.

'Well, well; you lead the way, and I'll engage that the master shall give me shelter and a supper tonight.'

'Eh, you can try him!' muttered my reluctant guide; and, still shaking his head, he hobbled, gnome-like, away through the falling snow. A large mass loomed up presently out of the darkness, and a huge dog rushed out, barking furiously.

'Is this the house?' I asked.

'Ay, it's the house. Down, Bey!' And he fumbled in his pocket for the key.

I drew up close behind him, prepared to lose no chance of entrance, and saw in the little circle of light shed by the lantern that the door was heavily studded with iron nails, like the door of a prison. In another minute he had turned the key and I had pushed past him into the house.

Once inside, I looked round with curiosity, and found myself in a great raftered hall, which served, apparently, a variety of uses. One end was piled to the roof with corn, like a barn. The other was stored with flour-sacks, agricultural implements, casks, and all kinds of miscellaneous lumber; while from the beams overhead hung rows of hams, flitches, and bunches of dried herbs for winter use. In the centre of the floor stood some huge object gauntly dressed in a dingy wrapping-cloth, and reaching halfway to the rafters. Lifting a corner of this cloth, I saw, to my surprise, a telescope of very considerable size, mounted on a rude movable platform, with four small wheels. The tube was made of painted wood, bound round with bands of metal rudely fashioned; the speculum, so far as I could estimate its size in the dim light, measured at least fifteen inches in diameter. While I was yet examining the instrument, and asking myself whether it was not the work of some self-taught optician, a bell rang sharply.

'That's for you,' said my guide, with a malicious grin. 'Yonder's his room.'

He pointed to a low black door at the opposite side of the hall. I crossed over, rapped somewhat loudly, and went in, without waiting for an invitation. A huge, white-haired old man rose from a table covered with books and papers, and confronted me sternly.

'Who are you?' said he. 'How came you here? What do you want?'

'James Murray, barrister-at-law. On foot across the moor. Meat, drink, and sleep.'

He bent his bushy brows into a portentous frown.

'Mine is not a house of entertainment,' he said, haughtily. 'Jacob, how dared you admit this stranger?'

'I didn't admit him,' grumbled the old man. 'He followed me over the muir, and shouldered his way in before me. I'm no match for six foot two.'

'And pray, sir, by what right have you forced an entrance into my house?'

'The same by which I should have clung to your boat, if I were drowning. The right of self-preservation.'

'Self-preservation?'

'There's an inch of snow on the ground already,' I replied, briefly; 'and it would be deep enough to cover my body before daybreak.'

He strode to the window, pulled aside a heavy black curtain, and looked out.

'It is true,' he said. 'You can stay, if you choose, till morning.

Jacob, serve the supper.'

With this he waved me to a seat, resumed his own, and became at once absorbed in the studies from which I had disturbed him.

I placed my gun in a corner, drew a chair to the hearth, and examined my quarters at leisure. Smaller and less incongruous in its arrangements than the hall, this room contained, nevertheless, much to awaken my curiosity. The floor was carpetless. The whitewashed walls were in parts scrawled over with strange diagrams, and in others covered with shelves crowded with philosophical instruments, the uses of many of which were unknown to me. On one side of the fireplace stood a bookcase filled with dingy folios; on the other, a small organ, fantastically decorated with painted carvings of medieval saints and devils. Through the half-opened door of a cupboard at the further end of the room, I saw a long array of geological specimens, surgical preparations, crucibles, retorts, and jars of chemicals; while on the mantelshelf beside me, amid a number of small objects, stood a model of the solar system, a small galvanic battery, and a microscope. Every chair had its burden. Every corner was heaped high with books. The very floor was littered over with maps, casts, papers, tracings, and learned lumber of all conceivable kinds.

I stared about me with an amazement increased by every fresh object upon which my eyes chanced to rest. So strange a room I had never seen; yet seemed it stranger still to find such a room in a lone farmhouse amid those wild and solitary moors! Over and over again, I looked from my host to his surroundings, and from his surroundings back to my host, asking myself who and what he could be? His head was singularly fine; but it was more the head of a poet than of a philosopher. Broad in the temples, prominent over the eyes, and clothed with a rough profusion of perfectly white hair, it had all the ideality and much of the ruggedness that characterises the head of Ludwig van Beethoven. There were the same deep lines about the mouth, and the same stern furrows in the brow. There was the same concentration of expression. While I was yet observing him, the door opened, and Jacob brought in the supper. His master then closed his book, rose, and with more courtesy of manner than he had yet shown, invited me to the table.

A dish of ham and eggs, a loaf of brown bread, and a bottle of admirable sherry, were placed before me.

'I have but the homeliest farmhouse fare to offer you, sir,' said my entertainer. 'Your appetite, I trust, will make up for the deficiencies of our larder.'

I had already fallen upon the viands, and now protested, with the enthusiasm of a starving sportsman, that I had never eaten anything so delicious.

He bowed stiffly, and sat down to his own supper, which consisted, primitively, of a jug of milk and a basin of porridge. We ate in silence, and, when we had done, Jacob removed the tray. I then drew my chair back to the fireside. My host, somewhat to my surprise, did the same, and turning abruptly towards me, said:

'Sir, I have lived here in strict retirement for three-and-twenty years. During that time, I have not seen as many strange faces, and I have not read a single newspaper. You are the first stranger who has crossed my threshold for more than four years. Will you favour me with a few words of information respecting that outer world from which I have parted company so long?'

'Pray interrogate me,' I replied. 'I am heartily at your service.'

He bent his head in acknowledgment; leaned forward, with his elbows resting on his knees and his chin supported in the palms of his hands; stared fixedly into the fire; and proceeded to question me.

His inquiries related chiefly to scientific matters, with the later progress of which, as applied to the practical purposes of life, he was almost wholly unacquainted. No student of science myself, I replied as well as my slight information permitted; but the task was far from easy, and I was much relieved when, passing from interrogation to discussion, he began pouring forth his own conclusions upon the facts which I had been attempting to place before him. He talked, and I listened spellbound. He talked till I believe he almost forgot my presence, and only thought aloud. I had never heard anything like it then; I have never heard anything like it since. Familiar with all systems of all philosophies, subtle in analysis, bold in generalization, he poured forth his thoughts in an uninterrupted stream, and, still leaning forward in the same moody attitude with his eyes fixed upon the fire, wandered from topic to topic, from speculation to speculation, like an inspired dreamer. From practical science to mental philosophy; from electricity in the wire to electricity in the nerve; from Watts to Mesmer, from Mesmer to Reichenbach, from Reichenbach to Swedenborg, Spinoza, Condillac, Descartes, Berkeley, Aristotle, Plato, and the Magi and mystics of the East, were transitions which, however bewildering in their variety and scope, seemed easy and harmonious upon his lips as sequences in music. By-and-by—I forget now by what link of conjecture or illustration—he passed on to that field which lies beyond the boundary line of even conjectural philosophy, and reaches no man knows whither. He spoke of the soul and its aspirations; of the spirit and its powers; of second sight; of prophecy; of those phenomena which, under the names of ghosts, spectres, and supernatural appearances, have been denied by the sceptics and attested by the credulous, of all ages.

'The world,' he said, 'grows hourly more and more sceptical

of all that lies beyond its own narrow radius; and our men of science foster the fatal tendency. They condemn as fable all that resists experiment. They reject as false all that cannot be brought to the test of the laboratory or the dissecting-room. Against what superstition have they waged so long and obstinate a war, as against the belief in apparitions? And yet what superstition has maintained its hold upon the minds of men so long and so firmly? Show me any fact in physics, in history, in archæology, which is supported by testimony so wide and so various. Attested by all races of men, in all ages, and in all climates, by the soberest sages of antiquity, by the rudest savage of today, by the Christian, the Pagan, the Pantheist, the Materialist, this phenomenon is treated as a nursery tale by the philosophers of our century. Circumstantial evidence weighs with them as a feather in the balance. The comparison of causes with effects, however valuable in physical science, is put aside as worthless and unreliable. The evidence of competent witnesses, however conclusive in a court of justice, counts for nothing. He who pauses before he pronounces, is condemned as a trifler. He who believes, is a dreamer or a fool.'

He spoke with bitterness, and, having said thus, relapsed for some minutes into silence. Presently he raised his head from his hands, and added, with an altered voice and manner, 'I, sir, paused, investigated, believed, and was not ashamed to state my convictions to the world. I, too, was branded as a visionary, held up to ridicule by my contemporaries, and hooted from that field of science in which I had laboured with honour during all the best years of my life. These things happened just three-and-twenty years ago. Since then, I have lived as you see me living now, and the world has forgotten me, as I have forgotten the world. You have my history.'

'It is a very sad one,' I murmured, scarcely knowing what to answer.

'It is a very common one,' he replied. 'I have only suffered for the truth, as many a better and wiser man has suffered before me.'

He rose, as if desirous of ending the conversation, and went over to the window.

'It has ceased snowing,' he observed, as he dropped the curtain, and came back to the fireside.

'Ceased!' I exclaimed, starting eagerly to my feet. 'Oh, if it were only possible—but no! It is hopeless. Even if I could find my way across the moor, I could not walk twenty miles tonight.'

'Walk twenty miles tonight!' repeated my host. 'What are you thinking of?'

'Of my wife,' I replied, impatiently. 'Of my young wife, who does not know that I have lost my way, and who is at this moment breaking her heart with suspense and terror.'

'Where is she?'

'At Dwolding, twenty miles away.'

'At Dwolding,' he echoed, thoughtfully. 'Yes, the distance, it is true, is twenty miles; but—are you so very anxious to save the next six or eight hours?'

'So very, very anxious, that I would give ten guineas at this moment for a guide and a horse.'

'Your wish can be gratified at a less costly rate,' said he, smiling. 'The night mail from the north, which changes horses at Dwolding, passes within five miles of this spot, and will be due at a certain crossroads in about an hour and a quarter. If Jacob were to go with you across the moor, and put you into the old coach-road, you could find your way, I suppose, to where it joins the new one?'

'Easily—gladly.'

He smiled again, rang the bell, gave the old servant his directions, and, taking a bottle of whisky and a wineglass from the cupboard in which he kept his chemicals, said:

'The snow lies deep, and it will be difficult walking tonight on the moor. A glass of usquebaugh before you start?'

I would have declined the spirit, but he pressed it on me, and I drank it. It went down my throat like liquid flame, and almost took my breath away.

'It is strong,' he said; 'but it will help to keep out the cold. And now you have no moments to spare. Goodnight!'

I thanked him for his hospitality, and would have shaken hands, but that he had turned away before I could finish my sentence. In another minute I had traversed the hall, Jacob had locked the outer door behind me, and we were out on the wide white moor.

Although the wind had fallen, it was still bitterly cold. Not a star glimmered in the black vault overhead. Not a sound, save the rapid crunching of the snow beneath our feet, disturbed the heavy stillness of the night. Jacob, not too well pleased with his mission, shambled on before in sullen silence, his lantern in his hand, and his shadow at his feet. I followed, with my gun over my shoulder, as little inclined for conversation as himself. My thoughts were full of my late host. His voice yet rang in my ears. His eloquence yet held my imagination captive. I remember to this day, with surprise, how my over-excited brain retained whole sentences and parts of sentences, troops of brilliant images, and fragments of splendid reasoning, in the very words in which he had uttered them. Musing thus over what I had heard, and striving to recall a lost link here and there, I strode on at the heels of my guide, absorbed and unobservant. Presently—at the end, as it seemed to me, of only a few minutes—he came to a sudden halt, and said:

'Yon's your road. Keep the stone fence to your right hand, and you can't fail of the way.'

'This, then, is the old coach-road?'

'Ay, 'tis the old coach-road.'

'And how far do I go, before I reach the crossroads?'

'Nigh upon three mile.'

I pulled out my purse, and he became more communicative.

'The road's a fair road enough,' said he, 'for foot passengers; but 'twas over steep and narrow for the northern traffic. You'll mind where the parapet's broken away, close again the signpost. It's never been mended since the accident.'

'What accident?'

'Eh, the night mail pitched right over into the valley below—a gude fifty feet an' more—just at the worst bit o' road in the whole county.'

'Horrible! Were many lives lost?'

'All. Four were found dead, and t'other two died next morning.'

'How long is it since this happened?'

'Just nine year.'

'Near the signpost, you say? I will bear it in mind. Goodnight.'

'Gude night, sir, and thankee.' Jacob pocketed his half-crown, made a faint pretence of touching his hat, and trudged back by the way he had come.

I watched the light of his lantern till it quite disappeared, and then turned to pursue my way alone. This was no longer matter of the slightest difficulty, for, despite the dead darkness overhead, the line of stone fence showed distinctly enough against the pale gleam of the snow. How silent it seemed now, with only my footsteps to listen to; how silent and how solitary! A strange disagreeable sense of loneliness stole over me. I walked faster. I hummed a fragment of a tune. I cast up enormous sums in my head, and accumulated them at compound interest. I did my best, in short, to forget the startling speculations to which I had but just been listening, and, to some extent, I succeeded.

Meanwhile, the night air seemed to become colder and colder, and though I walked fast I found it impossible to keep myself warm. My feet were like ice. I lost sensation in my hands, and grasped my gun mechanically. I even breathed with difficulty, as though, instead of traversing a quiet north country highway, I were scaling the uppermost heights of some gigantic Alp. This last symptom became presently so distressing, that I was forced to stop for a few minutes, and lean against the stone fence. As I did so, I chanced to look back up the road, and there, to my infinite relief, I saw a distant point of light, like the gleam of an approaching lantern. I at first concluded that Jacob had retraced his steps and followed me; but even as the conjecture presented itself, a second light flashed into sight—a light evidently parallel with the first, and approaching at the same rate of motion. It needed no second thought to show me that these must be the carriage-lamps of some private vehicle, though it seemed strange that any private vehicle should take a road professedly disused and dangerous

There could be no doubt, however, of the fact, for the lamps grew larger and brighter every moment, and I even fancied I could already see the dark outline of the carriage between them. It was coming up very fast, and quite noiselessly, the snow being nearly a foot deep under the wheels.

And now the body of the vehicle became distinctly visible behind the lamps. It looked strangely lofty. A sudden suspicion flashed upon me. Was it possible that I had passed the crossroads in the dark without observing the signpost, and could this be the very coach which I had come to meet?

No need to ask myself that question a second time, for here it came round the bend of the road, guard and driver, one outside passenger, and four steaming greys, all wrapped in a soft haze of light, through which the lamps blazed out, like a pair of fiery meteors.

I jumped forward, waved my hat, and shouted. The mail came down at full speed, and passed me. For a moment I feared that I had not been seen or heard, but it was only for a moment. The coachman pulled up; the guard, muffled to the eyes in capes and comforters, and apparently sound asleep in the rumble, neither answered my hail nor made the slightest effort to dismount; the outside passenger did not even turn his head. I opened the door for myself, and looked in. There were but three travellers inside, so I stepped in, shut the door, slipped into the vacant corner, and congratulated myself on my good fortune.

The atmosphere of the coach seemed, if possible, colder than that of the outer air, and was pervaded by a singularly damp and disagreeable smell. I looked round at my fellow-passengers. They were all three men, and all silent. They did not seem to be asleep, but each leaned back in his corner of the vehicle, as if absorbed in his own reflections. I attempted to open a conversation.

'How intensely cold it is tonight,' I said, addressing my opposite neighbour.

He lifted his head, looked at me, but made no reply.

'The winter,' I added, 'seems to have begun in earnest.'

Although the corner in which he sat was so dim that I could distinguish none of his features very clearly, I saw that his eyes were still turned full upon me. And yet he answered never a word.

At any other time I should have felt, and perhaps expressed, some annoyance, but at the moment I felt too ill to do either. The icy coldness of the night air had struck a chill to my very marrow, and the strange smell inside the coach was affecting me with an intolerable nausea. I shivered from head to foot, and, turning to my left-hand neighbour, asked if he had any objection to an open window?

He neither spoke nor stirred.

I repeated the question somewhat more loudly, but with the same result. Then I lost patience, and let the sash down. As I did so, the leather strap broke in my hand, and I observed that the glass was covered with a thick coat of mildew, the accumulation, apparently, of years. My attention being thus drawn to the condition of the coach, I examined it more narrowly, and saw by the uncertain light of the outer lamps that it was in the last stage of dilapidation. Every part of it was not only out of repair, but in a condition of decay. The sashes splintered at a touch. The leather fittings were crusted over with mould, and literally rotting from the woodwork. The floor was almost breaking away beneath my feet. The whole machine, in short, was foul with damp, and had evidently been dragged from some outhouse in which it had been mouldering away for years, to do another day or two of duty on the road.

I turned to the third passenger, whom I had not yet addressed, and hazarded one more remark.

'This coach,' I said, 'is in a deplorable condition. The regular mail, I suppose, is under repair?'

He moved his head slowly, and looked me in the face, without speaking a word. I shall never forget that look while I live. I turned cold at heart under it. I turn cold at heart even now when I recall it. His eyes glowed with a fiery unnatural lustre. His face was livid as the face of a corpse. His bloodless lips were drawn back as if in the agony of death, and showed the gleaming teeth between.

The words that I was about to utter died upon my lips,

and a strange horror—a dreadful horror—came upon me. My sight had by this time become used to the gloom of the coach, and I could see with tolerable distinctness. I turned to my opposite neighbour. He, too, was looking at me, with the same startling pallor in his face, and the same stony glitter in his eyes. I passed my hand across my brow. I turned to the passenger on the seat beside my own, and saw—oh Heaven! How shall I describe what I saw? I saw that he was no living man—that none of them were living men, like myself! A pale phosphorescent light—the light of putrefaction—played upon their awful faces; upon their hair, dank with the dews of the grave; upon their clothes, earth-stained and dropping to pieces; upon their hands, which were as the hands of corpses long buried. Only their eyes, their terrible eyes, were living; and those eyes were all turned menacingly upon me!

A shriek of terror, a wild unintelligible cry for help and mercy, burst from my lips as I flung myself against the door, and strove in vain to open it.

In that single instant, brief and vivid as a landscape beheld in the flash of summer lightning, I saw the moon shining down through a rift of stormy cloud—the ghastly signpost rearing its warning finger by the wayside—the broken parapet—the plunging horses—the black gulf below. Then, the coach reeled like a ship at sea. Then, came a mighty crash—a sense of crushing pain—and then, darkness.

It seemed as if years had gone by when I awoke one morning from a deep sleep, and found my wife watching by my bedside. I will pass over the scene that ensued, and give you, in half a dozen words, the tale she told me with tears of thanksgiving. I had fallen over a precipice, close against the junction of the old coach-road and the new, and had only been saved from certain death by lighting upon a deep snowdrift that had accumulated at the foot of the rock beneath. In this snowdrift I was discovered at daybreak, by a couple of shepherds, who carried me to the nearest shelter, and brought a surgeon to my aid. The surgeon found me in a state of raving delirium, with a broken arm and a compound fracture of the skull. The letters in my pocketbook showed my name and address; my wife was summoned to nurse me; and, thanks to youth and a fine constitution, I came out of danger at last. The place of my fall, I need scarcely say, was precisely that at which a frightful accident had happened to the north mail nine years before.

I never told my wife the fearful events which I have just related to you. I told the surgeon who attended me; but he treated the whole adventure as a mere dream born of the fever in my brain. We discussed the question over and over again, until we found that we could discuss it with temper no longer, and then we dropped it. Others may form what conclusions they please—I know that twenty years ago I was the fourth inside passenger in that Phantom Coach.

THE BEAST WITH FIVE FINGERS

W.F. Harvey

The story, I suppose, begins with Adrian Borlsover, whom I met when I was a little boy and he an old man. My father had called to appeal for a subscription, and before he left, Mr Borlsover laid his right hand in blessing on my head. I shall never forget the awe in which I gazed up at his face and realized for the first time that eyes might be dark and beautiful and shining, and yet not able to see.

For Adrian Borlsover was blind.

He was an extraordinary man, who came of an eccentric stock. Borlsover sons for some reason always seemed to marry very ordinary women, which perhaps accounted for the fact that no Borlsover had been a genius, and only one Borlsover had been mad. But they were great champions of little causes, generous patrons of odd sciences, founders of querulous sects, trustworthy guides to the bypath meadows of erudition.

Adrian was an authority on the fertilization of orchids. He had held at one time the family living at Borlsover Conyers, until a congenital weakness of the lungs obliged him to seek a less rigorous climate in the sunny south-coast watering-place where I had seen him. Occasionally, he would relieve one or other of the local clergy. My father described him as a fine preacher, who gave long and inspiring sermons from what many men would have considered unprofitable texts. 'An excellent proof,' he would add, 'of the truth of the doctrine of direct verbal inspiration.'

Adrian Borlsover was exceedingly clever with his hands. His penmanship was exquisite. He illustrated all his scientific papers, made his own woodcuts, and carved the reredos that is at present the chief feature of interest in the church at Borlsover Conyers. He had an exceedingly clever knack in cutting silhouettes for young ladies and paper pigs and cows for little children, and made more than one complicated wind instrument of his own devising.

When he was fifty years old, Adrian Borlsover lost his sight. In a wonderfully short time he adapted himself to the new conditions of life. He quickly learnt to read Braille. So marvellous indeed was his sense of touch, that he was still able to maintain his interest in botany. The mere passing of his long supple fingers over a flower was sufficient means for its identification, though occasionally he would use his lips. I have found several letters of his among my father's correspondence; in no case was there anything to show that he was afflicted with blindness, and this in spite of the fact that he exercised undue economy in the spacing of lines. Towards the close of his life, Adrian Borlsover was credited with the powers of touch that seemed almost uncanny. It has been said that he could tell at once the colour of a ribbon placed between his fingers. My father would neither confirm nor deny the story.

Adrian Borlsover was a bachelor. His elder brother, Charles, had married late in life, leaving one son, Eustace, who lived in the gloomy Georgian mansion at Borlsover Conyers, where he could work undisturbed in collecting material for his great book on heredity.

Like his uncle, he was a remarkable man. The Borlsovers had always been born naturalists, but Eustace possessed in a special degree the power of systematizing his knowledge. He had received his university education in Germany; and then, after post-graduate work in Vienna and Naples, had travelled for four years in South America and the East, getting together a huge store of material for a new study into the processes of variation.

He lived alone at Borlsover Conyers with Saunders, his secretary, a man who bore a somewhat dubious reputation in the district, but whose powers as a mathematician, combined with his business abilities, were invaluable to Eustace.

Uncle and nephew saw little of each other. The visits of Eustace were confined to a week in the summer or autumn—tedious weeks, that dragged almost as slowly as the bath-chair in which the old man was drawn along the sunny sea-front. In their way the two men were fond of each other, though their intimacy would, doubtless, have been greater, had they shared the same religious views. Adrian held to the old-fashioned evangelical dogmas of his early manhood; his nephew for many years had been thinking of embracing Buddhism. Both men possessed, too, the reticence the Borlsovers had always shown, and which their enemies sometimes called hypocrisy. With Adrian it was a reticence as to the things he had left undone; but with Eustace it seemed that the curtain which he was so careful to leave undrawn hid something more than a half-empty chamber.

Two years before his death, Adrian Borlsover developed, unknown to himself, the not uncommon power of automatic writing. Eustace made the discovery by accident. Adrian was sitting reading in bed, the forefinger of his left hand tracing the Braille characters, when his nephew noticed that a pencil the old man held in his right hand was moving slowly along the opposite page. He left his seat in the window and sat down beside the bed. The right hand continued to move, and now he could see plainly that they were letters and words which it was forming.

'Adrian Borlsover,' wrote the hand, 'Eustace Borlsover, Charles Borlsover, Francis Borlsover, Sigismund Borlsover, Adrian Borlsover, Eustace Borlsover, Saville Borlsover. B for Borlsover. Honesty is the Best Policy. Beautiful Belinda Borlsover.'

'What curious nonsense!' said Eustace to himself.

'King George ascended the throne in 1760,' wrote the hand. 'Crowd, a noun of multitude; a collection of individuals. Adrian Borlsover, Eustace Borlsover.'

'It seems to me,' said his uncle, closing the book, 'that you had much better make the most of the afternoon sunshine and take your walk now.'

'I think perhaps I will,' Eustace answered as he picked up the volume. 'I won't go far, and when I come back, I can read to you those articles in *Nature* about which we were speaking.'

He went along the promenade, but stopped at the first shelter, and, seating himself in the corner best protected from the wind, he examined the book at leisure. Nearly every page was scored with a meaningless jumble of pencil-marks; rows of capital letters, short words, long words, complete sentences, copy-book tags. The whole thing, in fact had the appearance of a copy-book, and, on a more careful scrutiny, Eustace thought that there was ample evidence to show that the handwriting at the beginning of the book, good though it was, was not nearly so good as the handwriting at the end.

He left his uncle at the end of October with a promise to return early in December. It seemed to him quite clear that the old man's power of automatic writing was developing rapidly, and for the first time he looked forward to a visit that would combine duty with interest.

But on his return he was at first disappointed. His uncle, he thought, looked older. He was listless, too, preferring others to read to him and dictating nearly all his letters. Not until the day before he left had Eustace an opportunity of observing Adrian Borlsover's new-found faculty.

The old man, propped up in bed with pillows, had sunk into a light sleep. His two hands lay on the coverlet, his left hand tightly clasping his right. Eustace took an empty manuscript-book and placed a pencil within reach of the fingers of the right hand. They snatched at it eagerly, then dropped the pencil to loose the left hand from its restraining grasp.

'Perhaps to prevent interference I had better hold that hand,' said Eustace to himself, as he watched the pencil. Almost immediately it began to write.

'Blundering Borlsovers, unnecessarily unnatural, extraordinarily eccentric, culpably curious.'

'Who are you?' asked Eustace in a low voice.

'Never you mind,' wrote the hand of Adrian.

'Is it my uncle who is writing?'

'O my prophetic soul, mine uncle!'

'Is it anyone I know?'

'Silly Eustace, you'll see me very soon.'

'When shall I see you?'

'When poor old Adrian's dead.'

'Where shall I see you?'

'Where shall you not?'

Instead of speaking his next question, Eustace wrote it. 'What is the time?'

The fingers dropped the pencil and moved three or four times across the paper. Then, picking up the pencil, they wrote: 'Ten minutes before four. Put your book away, Eustace. Adrian mustn't find us working at this sort of thing. He doesn't know what to make of it, and I won't have poor old Adrian disturbed. Au revoir!'

Adrian Borlsover awoke with a start.

'I've been dreaming again,' he said; 'such queer dreams of leaguered cities and forgotten towns. You were mixed up in this one, Eustace, though I can't remember how. Eustace, I want to warn you. Don't walk in doubtful paths. Choose your friends well. Your poor grandfather...'

A fit of coughing put an end to what he was saying, but Eustace saw that the hand was still writing. He managed unnoticed to draw the book away. 'I'll light the gas,' he said, 'and ring for tea.' On the other side of the bed-curtain he saw the last sentences that had been written.

'It's too late, Adrian,' he read. 'We're friends already, aren't we, Eustace Borlsover?'

On the following day Eustace left. He thought his uncle looked ill when he said goodbye, and the old man spoke despondently of the failure his life had been.

'Nonsense, uncle,' said his nephew. 'You have got over your difficulties in a way not one in a hundred thousand would have done. Everyone marvels at your splendid perseverance in teaching your hand to take the place of your lost sight. To me it's been a revelation of the possibilities of education.'

'Education,' said his uncle dreamily, as if the word had started a new train of thought. 'Education is good so long as you know to whom and for what purpose you give it. But with the lower orders of men, the base and more sordid spirits, I have grave doubts as to its results. Well, goodbye, Eustace; I may not see you again. You are a true Borlsover, with all the Borlsover faults. Marry, Eustace. Marry some good, sensible girl. And if by any chance I don't see you again, my will is at my solicitor's. I've not left you any legacy, because I know you're well-provided for; but I thought you might like to have my books. Oh, and there's just one other thing. You know, before the end people often lose control over themselves and make absurd requests. Don't pay any attention to them, Eustace. Goodbye!' and he held out his hand. Eustace took it. It remained in his a fraction of a second longer than he had expected and gripped him with a virility that was surprising. There was, too, in its touch a subtle sense of intimacy.

'Why, uncle,' he said, 'I shall see you alive and well for many long years to come.'

Two months later Adrian Borlsover died.

Eustace Borlsover was in Naples at the time. He read the obituary notice in the *Morning Post* on the day announced for the funeral.

'Poor old fellow!' he said. 'I wonder whether I shall find room for all his books.'

The question occurred to him again with greater force when three days later, he found himself standing in the library at Borlsover Conyers, a huge room built for use and not for beauty in the year of Waterloo by a Borlsover who was an ardent admirer of the great Napoleon. It was arranged on the plan of many college libraries, with tall projecting bookcases forming deep recesses of dusty silence, fit graves for the old hates of forgotten controversy, the dead passions of forgotten lives. At the end of the room, behind the bust of some unknown eighteenth-century divine, an ugly iron corkscrew stair led to a shelf-lined gallery. Nearly, every shelf was full.

'I must talk to Saunders about it,' said Eustace. 'I suppose that we shall have to have the billiard-room fitted up with bookcases.'

The two men met for the first time after many weeks in the dining-room that evening.

'Hallo!' said Eustace, standing before the fire with his hands in his pockets. 'How goes the world, Saunders? Why these dress togs?' He himself was wearing an old shooting-jacket. He did not believe in mourning, as he had told his uncle on his last visit; and, though he usually went in for quiet-coloured ties, he wore this evening one of an ugly red, in order to shock Morton, the butler, and to make them thrash out the whole question of mourning for themselves in the servants' hall. Eustace was a true Borlsover. 'The world,' said Saunders, 'goes the same as usual, confoundedly slow. The dress togs are accounted for by an invitation from Captain Lockwood to bridge.'

'How are you getting there?'

'There's something the matter with the car, so I've told Jackson to drive me round in the dogcart. Any objection?'

'O dear me, no! We've had all things in common for far too many years for me to raise objections at this hour of the day.'

'You'll find your correspondence in the library,' went on Saunders. 'Most of it I've seen to. There are a few private letters I haven't opened. There's also a box with a rat or something inside it that came by the evening post. Very likely it's the six-toed beast Terry was sending us to cross with the four-toed albino. I didn't look because I didn't want to mess up my things; but I should gather from the way it's jumping about that it's pretty hungry'

'Oh, I'll see to it,' said Eustace, 'while you and the captain earn an honest penny.'

Dinner over and Saunders gone, Eustace went into the library. Though the fire had been lit, the room was by no means cheerful.

'We'll have all the lights on, at any rate,' he said, as he turned the switches. 'And, Morton,' he added, when the butler brought the coffee, 'get me a screwdriver or something to undo this box. Whatever the animal is, he's kicking up the deuce of a row. What is it? Why are you dawdling?'

'If you please, sir, when the postman brought it, he told me that they'd bored the holes in the lid at the post office. There were no breathing holes in the lid, sir, and they didn't want the animal to die. That is all, sir.'

'It's culpably careless of the man, whoever he was,' said Eustace as he removed the screws, 'packing an animal like this in a wooden box with no means of getting air. Confound it all! I meant to ask Morton to bring me a cage to put it in. Now I suppose I shall have to get one myself.'

He placed a heavy book on the lid from which the screws had been removed, and went into the billiard-room. As he came back into the library with an empty cage in his hand, he heard the sound of something falling, and then of something scuttling along the floor.

'Bother it! The beast's got out. How in the world am I to find it again in this library?'

To search for it did indeed seem hopeless. He tried to follow the sound of the scuttling in one of the recesses, where the animal seemed to be running behind the books on the shelves; but it was impossible to locate it. Eustace resolved to go on quietly reading. Very likely the animal might gain confidence and show itself Saunders seemed to have dealt in his usual methodical manner with most of the correspondence. There were still the private letters.

What was that? Two sharp clicks and the lights in the hideous candelabra that hung from the ceiling suddenly went out.

'I wonder if something has gone wrong with the fuse,' said Eustace, as he went to the switches by the door. Then he stopped. There was a noise at the other end of the room, as if something was crawling up the iron corkscrew stair. 'If it's gone into the gallery,' he said, 'well and good.' He hastily turned on the lights, crossed the room, and climbed up the stair. But he could see nothing. His grandfather had placed a little gate at the top of the stair, so that children could run and romp in the gallery without fear of accident. This Eustace closed, and, having considerably narrowed the circle of his search, returned to his desk by the fire.

How gloomy the library was! There was no sense of intimacy about the room. The few busts that an eighteenth-century Borlsover had brought back from the grand tour might have been in keeping in the old library. Here they seemed out of place. They made the room feel cold in spite of the heavy red damask curtains and great gilt cornices.

With a crash two heavy books fell from the gallery to the floor; then, as Borlsover looked, another, and yet another.

'Very well. You'll starve for this, my beauty!' he said. 'We'll do some little experiments on the metabolism of rats deprived of water. Go on! Chuck them down! I think I've got the upper hand.' He turned once more to his correspondence. The letter was from the family solicitor. It spoke of his uncle's death, and of the valuable collection of books that had been left to him in the will.

'There was one request [he read] which certainly came as a surprise to me. As you know, Mr Adrian Borlsover had left instructions that his body was to be buried in as simple a manner as possible at Eastbourne. He expressed a desire that there should be neither wreaths nor flowers of any kind, and hoped that his friends and relatives would not consider it necessary to wear mourning. The day before his death we received a letter cancelling these instructions. He wished the body to be embalmed (he gave us the address of the man we were to employ—Pennifer, Ludgate Hill), with orders that his right hand should be sent to you stating that it was at your special request. The other arrangements about the funeral remained unaltered.'

'Good Lord,' said Eustace, 'what in the world was the old boy driving at? And what in the name of all that's holy is that?'

Someone was in the gallery. Someone had pulled the cord attached to one of the blinds, and it had rolled up with a snap. Someone must be in the gallery, for a second blind did the same. Someone must be walking round the gallery, for one after the other the blinds sprang up, letting in the moonlight.

'I haven't got to the bottom of this yet,' said Eustace, 'but I will do, before the night is very much older'; and he hurried up the corkscrew stair. He had just got to the top when the lights went out a second time, and he heard again the scuttling along the floor. Quickly he stole on tiptoe in the dim moonshine in the direction of the noise, feeling, as he went, for one of the switches. His fingers touched the metal knob at last. He turned on the electric light.

About ten yards in front of him, crawling along the floor, was a man's hand. Eustace stared at it in utter amazement. It was moving quickly in the manner of a geometer caterpillar, the fingers humped up one moment, flattened out the next; the thumb appeared to give a crablike motion all the while. While he was looking, too surprised to stir, the hand disappeared round the corner. Eustace ran forward. He no longer saw it, but he could hear it, as it squeezed its way behind the books on one of the shelves. A heavy volume had been displaced. There was a gap in the row of books, where it had got in. In his fear lest it should escape him again, he seized the first book that came to his hand and plugged it into the hole. Then, emptying two shelves of their contents, he took the wooden boards and propped them up in front to make his barrier doubly sure.

'I wish Saunders was back,' he said; 'one can't tackle this sort of thing alone.' It was after eleven, and there seemed little likelihood of Saunders returning before twelve. He did not dare to leave the shelf unwatched, even to run downstairs to ring the bell. Morton, the butler, often used to come round about eleven to see that the windows were fastened, but he might not come. Eustace was thoroughly unstrung. At last he heard steps down below.

'Morton!' he shouted. 'Morton!'

'Sir?'

'Has Mr Saunders got back yet?'

'Not yet, sir.'

'Well, bring me some brandy, and hurry up about it. I'm up in the gallery, you duffer.'

'Thanks,' said Eustace, as he emptied the glass. 'Don't go to bed yet, Morton. There are a lot of books that have fallen down by accident. Bring them up and put them back on their shelves.'

Morton had never seen Borlsover in so talkative a mood as on that night. 'Here,' said Eustace, when the books had been put back and dusted, 'you might hold up these boards for me, Morton. That beast in the box got out, and I've been chasing it all over the place.'

'I think I can hear it chewing at the books, sir. They're not valuable, I hope? I think that's the carriage, sir; I'll go and call Mr Saunders.'

It seemed to Eustace that he was away for five minutes, but it could hardly have been more than one, when he returned with Saunders. 'All right, Morton, you can go now. I'm up here, Saunders.'

'What's all the row?' asked Saunders, as he lounged forward with his hands in his pockets. The luck had been with him all the evening. He was completely satisfied, both with himself and with Captain Lockwood's taste in wines. 'What's the matter? You look to me to be in an absolutely blue funk.'

'That old devil of an uncle of mine,' began Eustace—'Oh, I can't explain it all. It's his hand that's been playing Old Harry all the evening. But I've got it cornered behind these books. You've got to help me to catch it.'

'What's up with you, Eustace? What's the game?'

'It's no game, you silly idiot! If you don't believe me, take out one of those books and put your hand in and feel.'

'All right,' said Saunders; 'but wait till I've rolled up my sleeve. The accumulated dust of centuries, eh?' He took off his coat, knelt down, and thrust his arm along the shelf.

'There's something there right enough,' he said. 'It's got a funny, stumpy end to it, whatever it is, and nips like a crab. Ah! no, you don't!' He pulled his hand out in a flash. 'Shove in a book quickly. Now it can't get out.'

'What was it?' asked Eustace.

'Something that wanted very much to get hold of me. I felt what seemed like a thumb and forefinger. Give me some brandy.'

'How are we to get it out of there?'

'What about a landing-net?'

'No good. It would be too smart for us. I tell you, Saunders, it can cover the ground far faster than I can walk. But I think I see how we can manage it. The two books at the end of the shelf are big ones, that go right back against the wall. The others are very thin. I'll take out one at a time, and you slide the rest along, until we have it squashed between the end two.'

It certainly seemed to be the best plan. One by one as they took out the books, the space behind grew smaller and smaller. There was something in it that was certainly very much alive. Once they caught sight of fingers feeling for a way of escape. At last they had it pressed between the two big books.

'There's muscle there, if there isn't warm flesh and blood,' said Saunders, as he held them together. 'It seems to be a hand right enough, too. I suppose this is a sort of infectious hallucination. I've read about such cases before.'

'Infectious fiddlesticks!' said Eustace, his face white with anger; 'bring the thing downstairs. We'll get it back into the box.'

It was not altogether easy, but they were successful at last. 'Drive in the screws,' said Eustace; 'we won't run any risks. Put the box in this old desk of mine. There's nothing in it that I want. Here's the key. Thank goodness there's nothing wrong with the lock.'

'Quite a lively evening,' said Saunders. 'Now let's hear more about your uncle.'

They sat up together until early morning. Saunders had no desire for sleep. Eustace was trying to explain and to forget; to conceal from himself a fear that he had never felt before—the fear of walking alone down the long corridor to his bedroom.

'Whatever it was,' said Eustace to Saunders on the following morning, 'I propose that we drop the subject. There's nothing to keep us here for the next ten days. We'll motor up to the Lakes and get some climbing.'

'And see nobody all day, and sit bored to death with each other every night. Not for me, thanks. Why not run up to town? Run's the exact word in this case, isn't it? We're both in such a blessed funk. Pull yourself together, Eustace, and let's have another look at the hand.'

'As you like,' said Eustace; 'there's the key.'

They went into the library and opened the desk. The box was as they had left it on the previous night.

'What are you waiting for?' asked Eustace.

'I am waiting for you to volunteer to open the lid. However since you seem to funk it, allow me. There doesn't seem to be the likelihood of any rumpus this morning at all events.' He opened the lid and picked out the hand.

'Cold?' asked Eustace.

'Tepid. A bit below blood heat by the feel. Soft and supple too. If it's the embalming, it's a sort of embalming I've never seen before. Is it your uncle's hand?'

'Oh yes, it's his all right,' said Eustace. 'I should know those long thin fingers anywhere. Put it back in the box, Saunders. Never mind about the screws. I'll lock the desk, so that there'll be no chance of its getting out. We'll compromise by motoring up to town for a week. If we can get off soon after lunch, we ought to be at Grantham or Stamford by night.'

'Right,' said Saunders, 'and tomorrow—oh, well, by tomorrow we shall have forgotten all about this beastly thing.'

If, when the morrow came, they had not forgotten, it was certainly true that at the end of the week they were able to tell a very vivid ghost-story at the little supper Eustace gave on Halloween.

'You don't want us to believe that it's true, Mr Borlsover? How perfectly awful!'

'I'll take my oath on it, and so would Saunders here; wouldn't you, old chap?'

'Any number of oaths,' said Saunders. 'It was a long thin hand, you know, and it gripped me just like that.'

'Don't, Mr Saunders! Don't! How perfectly horrid! Now tell us another one, do! Only a really creepy one, please.'

'Here's a pretty mess!' said Eustace on the following day, as he threw a letter across the table to Saunders. 'It's your affair, though. Mrs Merrit, if I understand it, gives a month's notice.'

'Oh, that's quite absurd on Mrs Merrit's part,' replied Saunders. 'She doesn't know what she's talking about. Let's see what she says.'

Dear Sir [he read]. This is to let you know that I must give you a month's notice as from Tuesday, the 13th. For a long time I've felt the place too big for me; but when Jane Parfit and Emma Laidlaw go off with scarcely as much as an "If you please", after frightening the wits out of the other girls, so that they can't turn out a room by themselves or walk alone down the stairs for fear of treading on half-frozen toads or hearing it run along the passages at night, all I can say is that it's no place for me. So I must ask you, Mr Borlsover, sir, to find a new housekeeper, that has no objection to large and lonely houses, which some people do say, not that I believe them for a minute, my poor mother always having been a Wesleyan, are haunted.

Yours faithfully,

Elizabeth Merrit.

PS.—I should be obliged if you would give my respects to Mr Saunders. I hope that he won't run any risks with his cold.

'Saunders,' said Eustace, 'you've always had a wonderful way with you in dealing with servants. You mustn't let poor old Merrit go.'

'Of course she shan't go,' said Saunders. 'She's probably only angling for a rise in salary. I'll write to her this morning.'

'No. There's nothing like a personal interview. We've had enough of town. We'll go back tomorrow, and you must work your cold for all it's worth. Don't forget that it's got on to the chest, and will require weeks of feeding up and nursing.'

'All right; I think I can manage Mrs Merrit.'

But Mrs Merrit was more obstinate than he had thought. She was very sorry to hear of Mr Saunders's cold, and how he lay awake all night in London coughing; very sorry indeed.

She'd change his room for him, gladly, and get the south room aired, and wouldn't he have a hot basin of bread and milk last thing at night? But she was afraid that she would have to leave at the end of the month.

'Try her with an increase of salary,' was the advice of Eustace.

It was no use. Mrs Merrit was obdurate, though she knew of a Mrs Goddard, who had been housekeeper to Lord Gargrave, who might be glad to come at the salary mentioned.

'What's the matter with the servants, Morton?' asked Eustace that evening, when he brought the coffee into the library. 'What's all this about Mrs Merrit wanting to leave?'

'If you please, sir, I was going to mention it myself. I have a confession to make, sir. When I found your note, asking me to open that desk and take out the box with the rat, I broke the lock, as you told me, and was glad to do it, because I could hear the animal in the box making a great noise, and I thought it wanted food. So I took out the box, sir, and got a cage, and was going to transfer it, when the animal got away.'

'What in the world are you talking about? I never wrote any such note.'

'Excuse me, sir; it was the note I picked up here on the floor on the day you and Mr Saunders left. I have it in my pocket now.'

It certainly seemed to be in Eustace's handwriting. It was written in pencil, and began somewhat abruptly.

'Get a hammer, Morton,' he read, 'or some other tool and break open the lock in the old desk in the library. Take out the box that is inside. You need not do anything else. The lid is already open. Eustace Borlsover.'

'And you opened the desk?'

'Yes, sir; and, as I was getting the cage ready, the animal hopped out.'

'What animal?'

'The animal inside the box, sir.'

'What did it look like?'

'Well, sir, I couldn't tell you,' said Morton nervously. 'My back was turned, and it was halfway down the room when I looked up.'

'What was its colour?' asked Saunders. 'Black?'

'Oh no, sir; a greyish white. It crept along in a very funny way, sir. I don't think it had a tail.'

'What did you do then?'

'I tried to catch it; but it was no use. So I set the rat-traps and kept the library shut. Then that girl, Emma Laidlaw, left the door open when she was cleaning, and I think it must have escaped.'

And you think it is the animal that's been frightening the maids?'

'Well, no sir, not quite. They said it was—you'll excuse me sir—a hand that they saw. Emma trod on it once at the bottom of the stairs. She thought then it was a half-frozen toad, only white. And then Parfit was washing up the dishes in the scullery. She wasn't thinking about anything in particular. It was close on dusk. She took her hands out of the water and was drying them absent-minded like on the roller towel, when she found she was drying someone else's hand as well, only colder than hers.'

'What nonsense!' exclaimed Saunders.

'Exactly sir; that's what I told her; but we couldn't get her to stop.'

'You don't believe all this?' said Eustace, turning suddenly towards the butler.

'Me, sir? Oh no, sir! I've not seen anything.'

'Nor heard anything?'

'Well, sir, if you must know, the bells do ring at odd times, and there's nobody there when we go; and when we go round to draw the blinds of a night, as often as not somebody's been there before us. But, as I says to Mrs Merrit, a young monkey might do wonderful things, and we all know that Mr Borlsover has had some strange animals about the place.'

'Very well, Morton, that will do.'

'What do you make of it?' asked Saunders, when they were alone. 'I mean of the letter he said you wrote.'

'Oh, that's simple enough,' said Eustace. 'See the paper it's written on? I stopped using that paper years ago, but there were a few odd sheets and envelopes left in the old desk. We never fastened up the lid of the box before locking it in. The hand got out, found a pencil, wrote this note, and shoved it through the crack on to the floor, where Morton found it. That's plain as daylight.'

'But the hand couldn't write!'

'Couldn't it? You've not seen it do the things I've seen.'

And he told Saunders more of what had happened at Eastbourne.

'Well,' said Saunders, 'in that case we have at least an explanation of the legacy. It was the hand which wrote, unknown to your uncle, that letter to your solicitor bequeathing itself to you. Your uncle had no more to do with that request than I. In fact, it would seem that he had some idea of this automatic writing and feared it.'

'Then if it's not my uncle, what is it?'

'I suppose some people might say that a disembodied spirit had got your uncle to educate and prepare a little body for it. Now it's got into that little body and is off on its own.'

'Well, what are we to do?'

'We'll keep our eyes open,' said Saunders, 'and try to catch it. If we can't do that, we shall have to wait till the bally clockwork runs down. After all, if it's flesh and blood, it can't live forever.'

For two days nothing happened. Then Saunders saw it sliding down the banister in the hall. He was taken unawares and lost a full second before he started in pursuit, only to find that the thing had escaped him. Three days later Eustace, writing alone in the library at night, saw it sitting on an open book at the other end of the room. The fingers crept over the page, as if it were reading; but before he had time to get up from his seat, it had taken the alarm, and was pulling itself up the curtains. Eustace watched it grimly, as it hung on to the cornice with three fingers and flicked thumb and forefinger at him in an expression of scornful derisio.

'I know what I'll do,' he said. 'If I only get it into the open I'll set the dogs on to it.'

He spoke to Saunders of the suggestion.

'It's a jolly good idea,' he said; 'only we won't wait till we find it out of doors. We'll get the dogs. There are the two terriers and the under-keeper's Irish mongrel, that's on to rats like a flash. Yom-spaniel has not got spirit enough for this sort of game.'

They brought the dogs into the house, and the keeper's Irish mongrel chewed up the slippers, and the terriers tripped up Morton as he waited at table; but all three were welcome. Even false security is better than no security at all.

For a fortnight nothing happened. Then the hand was caught not by the dogs, but by Mrs Merrit's grey parrot. The bird was in the habit of periodically removing the pins that kept its seed- and water-tin in place, and of escaping through the holes in the side of the cage. When once at liberty, Peter would show no inclination to return, and would often be about the house for days. Now, after six consecutive weeks of captivity, Peter had again discovered a new way of unloosing his bolts and was, at large, exploring the tapestried forests of the curtains and singing songs in praise of liberty from cornice and picture rail.

'It's no use your trying to catch him,' said Eustace to Mrs Merrit, as she came into the study one afternoon towards dusk with a step-ladder. 'You'd much better leave Peter alone. Starve him into surrender, Mrs Merrit; and don't leave bananas and seed about for him to peck at when he fancies he's hungry. You're far too soft-hearted.'

'Well, sir, I see he's right out of reach now on that picture-rail; so if you wouldn't mind closing the door, sir, when you leave the room, I'll bring his cage in tonight and put some meat inside it. He's that fond of meat, though it does make him pull out his feathers to suck the quills. They *do* say that if you cook—'

'Never mind, Mrs Merrit,' said Eustace, who was busy writing; 'that will do; I'll keep an eye on the bird.'

For a short time there was silence in the room.

'Scratch poor Peter,' said the bird. 'Scratch poor old Peter!'

'Be quiet, you beastly bird!'

'Poor old Peter! Scratch poor Peter; do!'

'I'm more likely to wring your neck, if I get hold of you.' He looked up at the picture-rail, and there was the hand, holding on to a hook with three fingers, and slowly scratching the head of the parrot with the fourth. Eustace ran to the bell and pressed it hard; then across to the window, which he closed with a bang. Frightened by the noise, the parrot shook its wings preparatory to flight, and, as it did so, the fingers of the hand got hold of it by the throat. There was a shrill scream from Peter, as he fluttered across the room, wheeling round in circles that ever descended, borne down under the weight that clung to him. The bird dropped at last quite suddenly, and Eustace saw fingers and feathers rolled into an inextricable mass on the floor. The struggle abruptly ceased, as finger and thumb squeezed the neck; the bird's eyes rolled up to show the white, and there was a faint, half-choked gurgle. But, before the fingers had time to loose their hold, Eustace had them in his own.

'Send Mr Saunders here at once,' he said to the maid who came in answer to the bell. 'Tell him I want him immediately.'

Then he went with the hand to the fire. There was a ragged gash across the back, where the bird's beak had torn it, but no blood oozed from the wound. He noted with disgust that the nails had grown long and discoloured.

'I'll burn the beastly thing,' he said. But he could not burn it He tried to throw it into the flames, but his own hands, as if impelled by some old primitive feeling, would not let him. And so Saunders found him, pale and irresolute, with the hand still clasped tightly in his fingers.

'I've got it at last,' he said, in a tone of triumph.

'Good, let's have a look at it.'

'Not when it's loose. Get me some nails and a hammer and a board of some sort.'

'Can you hold it all right?'

'Yes, the thing's quite limp; tired out with throttling poor old Peter, I should say.'

'And now,' said Saunders, when he returned with the things, 'what are we going to do?'

'Drive a nail through it first, so that it can't get away. Then we can take our time over examining it.'

'Do it yourself,' said Saunders. 'I don't mind helping you with guinea-pigs occasionally, when there's something to be learned, partly because I don't fear a guinea-pig's revenge. This thing's different.'

'Oh, my aunt!' he giggled hysterically, 'look at it now.' For the hand was writhing in agonized contortions, squirming and wriggling upon the nail like a worm upon the hook.

'Well,' said Saunders, 'you've done it now. I'll leave you to examine it.'

'Don't go, in heaven's name! Cover it up, man; cover it up! Shove a cloth over it! Here!' and he pulled off the antimacassar from the back of a chair and wrapped the board in it. 'Now get the keys from my pocket and open the safe. Chuck the other things out. Oh, Lord, it's getting itself into frightful knots! Open it quick!' He threw the thing in and banged the door.

'We'll keep it there till it dies,' he said. 'May I burn in hell, if I ever open the door of that safe again.'

Mrs Merrit departed at the end of the month. Her successor, Mrs Handyside, certainly was more successful in the management of the servants. Early in her rule she declared that she would stand no nonsense, and gossip soon withered and died.

'I shouldn't be surprised if Eustace married one of these days,' said Saunders. 'Well, I'm in no hurry for such an event. I know him far too well for the future Mrs Borlsover to like me. It will be the same old story again; a long friendship slowly made—marriage—and a long friendship quickly forgotten.'

But Eustace did not follow the advice of his uncle and marry. Old habits crept over and covered his new experience. He was, if anything, less morose, and showed a great inclination to take his natural part in country society.

Then came the burglary. The man, it was said, broke into the house by way of the conservatory. It was really little more than an attempt, for they only succeeded in carrying away a few pieces of plate from the pantry. The safe in the study was certainly found open and empty, but, as Mr Borlsover informed the police inspector, he had kept nothing of value in it during the last six months.

'Then you're lucky in getting off so easily, sir,' the man

replied. 'By the way they have gone about their business I should say the were experienced cracksmen. They must have caught the alarm when they were just beginning their evening's work.'

'Yes,' said Eustace, 'I suppose I am lucky.'

'I've no doubt,' said the inspector, 'that we shall be able to trace the men. I've said that they must have been old hands at the game. The way they got in and opened the safe shows that. But there's one little thing that puzzles me. One of them was careless enough not to wear gloves, and I'm bothered if I know what he was trying to do. I've traced his finger-marks on the new varnish on the window-sashes in every one of the downstairs rooms. They are very distinctive ones too.'

'Right hand or left or both?' asked Eustace.

'Oh, right every time. That's the funny thing. He must have been a foolhardy fellow, and I rather think it was him that wrote that.' He took out a slip of paper from his pocket. 'That's what he wrote, sir: "I've got out, Eustace Borlsover, but I'll be back before long." Some jailbird just escaped, I suppose. It will make it all the easier for us to trace him. Do you know the writing, sir?'

'No,' said Eustace. 'It's not the writing of anyone I know.'

'I'm not going to stay here any longer,' said Eustace to Saunders at luncheon. 'I've got on far better during the last six months than I expected, but I'm not going to run the risk of seeing that thing again. I shall go up to town this afternoon. Get Morton to put my things together, and join me with the car at Brighton on the day after tomorrow. And bring the proofs of those two papers with you. We'll run over them together.'

'How long are you going to be away?'

'I can't say for certain, but be prepared to stay for some time. We've stuck to work pretty closely through the summer, and I for one need a holiday. I'll engage the rooms at Brighton.

You'll find it best to break the journey at Hitchin. I'll wire to you there at the "Crown" to tell you the Brighton address.'

The house he chose at Brighton was in a terrace. He had been there before. It was kept by his old college gyp, a man of discreet silence, who was admirably partnered by an excellent cook. The rooms were on the first floor. The two bedrooms were at the back, and opened out of each other. 'Mr Saunders can have the smaller one, though it is the only one with a fire-place,' he said. 'I'll stick to the larger of the two, since it's got a bathroom adjoining. I wonder what time he'll arrive with the car.'

Saunders came about seven, cold and cross and dirty. 'We'll light the fire in the dining-room,' said Eustace, 'and get Prince to unpack some of the things while we are at dinner. What were the roads like?'

'Rotten. Swimming with mud, and a beastly cold wind against us all day. And this is July. Dear Old England!'

'Yes,' said Eustace, 'I think we might do worse than leave Old England for a few months.'

They turned in soon after twelve.

'You oughtn't to feel cold, Saunders,' said Eustace, 'when you can afford to sport a great fur-lined coat like this. 'You do yourself very well, all things considered. Look at those gloves, for instance. Who could possibly feel cold when wearing them?'

'They are far too clumsy, though, for driving. Try them on and see,' and he tossed them through the door on to Eustace's bed and went on with his unpacking. A minute later he heard a shrill cry of terror. 'Oh, Lord,' he heard, 'it's in the glove! Quick, Saunders quick!' Then came a smacking thud. Eustace had thrown it from him. 'I've chucked it into the bathroom,' he gasped; 'it's hit the wall and fallen into the bath. Come now, if you want to help,' Saunders, with a lighted candle in his hand, looked over the edge of the bath. There it was, old and maimed, dumb and blind, with a ragged hole in the middle, crawling, staggering, trying to creep up the slippery sides, only to fall back helpless.

'Stay there,' said Saunders. 'I'll empty a collar-box or something and we'll jam it in. It can't get out while I'm away.'

'Yes, it can,' shouted Eustace. 'It's getting out now; it's climbing up the plug-chain.—No, you brute, you filthy brute, you don't!—Come back, Saunders; it's getting away from me. I can't hold it; it's all slippery. Curse its claws! Shut the window, you idiot! It's got out!' There was the sound of something dropping on to the hard flag-stones below, and Eustace fell back fainting.

For a fortnight he was ill.

'I don't know what to make of it,' the doctor said to Saunders. 'I can only suppose that Mr Borlsover has suffered some great emotional shock. You had better let me send someone to help you nurse him. And by all means indulge that whim of his never to be left alone in the dark. I would keep a light burning all night, if I were you. But he *must* have more fresh air. It's perfectly absurd, this hatred of open windows.'

Eustace would have no one with him but Saunders. 'I don't want the other man,' he said. 'They'd smuggle it in somehow. I know they would.'

'Don't worry about it, old chap. This sort of thing can't go on indefinitely. You know I saw it this time as well as you. It wasn't half so active. It won't go on living much longer, especially after that fall. I heard it hit the flags myself. As soon as you're a bit stronger, we'll leave this place, not bag and baggage, but with only the clothes on our backs, so that it won't be able to hide anywhere. We'll escape it that way. We won't give any address, and we won't have any parcels sent after us. Cheer up, Eustace! You'll be well-enough to leave in a day or two. The doctor says I can take you out in a chair tomorrow.'

'What have I done?' asked Eustace. 'Why does it come after me? I'm no worse than other men. I'm no worse than you, Saunders; you know I'm not. It was you who was at the bottom of that dirty business in San Diego, and that was fifteen years ago.'

'It's not that, of course,' said Saunders. 'We are in the twentieth century, and even the parsons have dropped the idea of your old sins finding you out. Before you caught the hand in the library, it was filled with pure malevolence—to you and all mankind. After you spiked it through with that nail, it naturally forgot about other people and concentrated its attention on you. It was shut up in that safe, you know, for nearly six months. That gives plenty of time for thinking of revenge.'

Eustace Borlsover would not leave his room, but he thought there might be something in Saunders's suggestion of a sudden departure from Brighton. He began rapidly to regain his strength.

'We'll go on the first of September,' he said.

The evening of the thirty-first of August was oppressively warm. Though at midday the windows had been wide open, they had been shut an hour or so before dusk. Mrs Prince had long since ceased to wonder at the strange habits of the gentlemen on the first floor. Soon after their arrival she had been told to take down the heavy window curtains in the two bedrooms, and day by day the rooms had seemed to grow more bare. Nothing was left lying about.

'Mr Borlsover doesn't like to have any place where dirt can collect,' Saunders had said as an excuse. 'He likes to see into all the corners of the room.'

'Couldn't I open the window just a little?' he said to Eustace that evening. 'We're simply roasting in here, you know.'

'No, leave well alone. We're not a couple of boarding-school misses fresh from a course of hygiene lectures. Get the chess-board out.'

They sat down and played. At ten o'clock Mrs Prince came to the door with a note. 'I am sorry I didn't bring it before,' she said, 'but it was left in the letter-box.'

'Open it, Saunders, and see if it wants answering.'

It was very brief. There was neither address nor signature. 'Will eleven o'clock tonight be suitable for our last appointment?'

'Who is it from?' asked Borlsover.

'It was meant for me,' said Saunders. 'There's no answer, Mrs Prince,' and he put the paper into his pocket.

'A dunning letter from a tailor; I suppose he must have got wind of our leaving.'

It was a clever lie, and Eustace asked no more questions. They went on with their game.

On the landing outside Saunders could hear the grandfather's clock whispering the seconds, blurting out the quarter-hours.

'Check,' said Eustace. The clock struck eleven. At the same time there was a gentle knocking on the door; it seemed to come from the bottom panel.

'Who's there?' asked Eustace.

There was no answer.

'Mrs Prince, is that you?'

'She is up above,' said Saunders; 'I can hear her walking about the room.'

'Then lock the door; bolt it too. Your move, Saunders.'

While Saunders sat with his eyes on the chess-board, Eustace walked over to the window and examined the fastenings. He did the same in Saunders's room, and the bathroom. There were no doors between the three rooms, or he would have shut and locked them too.

'Now, Saunders,' he said, 'don't stay all night over your move. I've had time to smoke one cigarette already. It's bad to keep an invalid waiting. There's only one possible thing for you to do. What was that?'

'The ivy blowing against the window. There, it's your move now, Eustace.'

'It wasn't the ivy, you idiot! It was someone tapping at the window,' and he pulled up the blind. On the outer side of the window, clinging to the sash, was the hand.

'What is it that it's holding?'

'It's a pocket-knife. It's going to try to open the window by pushing back the fastener with the blade.'

'Well, let it try,' said Eustace. 'Those fasteners screw down; they can't be opened that way. Anyhow, we'll close the shutters. It's your move, Saunders; I've played.'

But Saunders found it impossible to fix his attention on the game. He could not understand Eustace, who seemed all at once to have lost his fear. 'What do you say to some wine?' he asked. 'You seem to be taking things coolly, but I don't mind confessing that I'm in a blessed funk.'

'You've no need to be. There's nothing supernatural about that hand, Saunders. I mean it seems to be governed by the laws of time and space. It's not the sort of thing that vanishes into thin air or slides through oaken doors. And since that's so, I defy it to get in here. We'll leave the place in the morning. I for one have bottomed the depths of fear. Fill your glass, man! The windows are all shuttered; the door is locked and bolted. Pledge me my Uncle Adrian! Drink, man! What are you waiting for?'

Saunders was standing with his glass half raised. 'It can get in,' he said hoarsely; 'it can get in. We've forgotten. There's the fireplace in my bedroom. It will come down the chimney.'

'Quick!' said Eustace, as he rushed into the other room; 'we haven't a minute to lose. What can we do? Light the fire, Saunders. Give me a match, quick!'

'They must be all in the other room. I'll get them.'

'Hurry, man, for goodness' sake! Look in the bookcase! Look in the bathroom! Here, come and stand here; I'll look.'

'Be quick!' shouted Saunders. 'I can hear something!'

'Then plug a sheet from your bed up the chimney. No, here's a match!' He had found one at last that had slipped into a crack in the floor.

'Is the fire laid? Good, but it may not burn. I know—the oil from that old reading-lamp and this cotton-wool. Now the match, quick! Pull the sheet away, you fool! We don't want it now.'

There was a great roar from the grate, as the flames shot up. Saunders had been a fraction of a second too late with the sheet. The oil had fallen on to it. It, too, was burning.

'The whole place will be on fire!' cried Eustace, as he tried to beat out the flames with a blanket. 'It's no good! I can't manage it. You must open the door, Saunders, and get help.'

Saunders ran to the door and fumbled with the bolts. The key was stiff in the lock. 'Hurry,' shouted Eustace, 'or the heat will be too much for me.' The key turned in the lock at last. For half a second Saunders stopped to look back. Afterwards he could never be quite sure as to what he had seen, but at the time he thought that something black and charred was creeping slowly, very slowly, from the mass of flames towards Eustace Borlsover. For a moment he thought of returning to his friend; but the noise and the smell of the burning sent him running down the passage, crying: 'Fire! Fire!' He rushed to the telephone to summon help, and then back to the bathroom—he should have thought of that before—for water. As he burst into the bedroom there came a scream of terror which ended suddenly, and then the sound of a heavy fall.

This is the story which I heard on successive Saturday evenings from the senior mathematical master at a second-rate suburban school. For Saunders has had to earn a living in a way which other men might reckon less congenial than his old manner of life. I had mentioned by chance the name of Adrian Borlsover, and wondered at the time why he changed the conversation with such unusual abruptness. A week later Saunders began to tell me something of his own history; sordid enough, though shielded with a reserve I could well understand, for it had to cover not only his failings, but those of a dead friend. Of the final tragedy he was at first especially loath to speak; and it was only gradually that I was able to piece together the narrative of the preceding pages. Saunders was reluctant to draw any conclusions. At one time he thought that the fingered beast had been animated by the spirit of Sigismund Borlsover, a sinister eighteenth-century ancestor, who, according to legend, built and worshipped in the ugly pagan temple that overlooked the lake. At another time Saunders believed the spirit to belong to a man whom Eustace had once employed as a laboratory assistant, 'a black-haired, spiteful little brute,' he said, 'who died cursing his doctor, because the fellow couldn't help him to live to settle some paltry score with Borlsover.'

From the point of view of direct contemporary evidence, Saunders's story is practically uncorroborated. All the letters mentioned in the narrative were destroyed, with the exception of the last note which Eustace received, or rather which he would have received, had not Saunders intercepted it. That I have seen myself. The handwriting was thin and shaky, the handwriting of an old man. I remember the Greek V was used in 'appointment'. A little thing that amused me at the time was that Saunders seemed to keep the note pressed between the pages of his Bible.

I had seen Adrian Borlsover once. Saunders I learnt to know well. It was by chance, however, and not by design, that I met a third person of the story, Morton, the butler. Saunders and I were walking in the Zoological Gardens one Sunday afternoon, when he called my attention to an old man who was standing before the door of the Reptile House.

'Why, Morton,' he said, clapping him on the back, 'how is the world treating you?'

'Poorly, Mr Saunders,' said the old fellow, though his face lighted up at the greeting. 'The winters drag terribly nowadays. There don't seem no summers or springs.'

'You haven't found what you were looking for, I suppose?'

'No, sir, not yet; but I shall some day. I always told them that Mr Borlsover kept some queer animals.'

'And what is he looking for?' I asked, when we had parted from him.

'A beast with five fingers,' said Saunders. 'This afternoon, since he has been in the Reptile House, I suppose it will be a reptile with a hand. Next week it will be a monkey with practically no body. The poor old chap is a born materialist.'

THE LAUGHING SKULL

Ruskin Bond

I am not normally bothered by skeletons and old bones—they are, after all, just the chalky remains of the long dead—so when my nephew Anil came back from medical college with a well-preserved skull, it was no cause for alarm. He was a second year student, at times a bit of a prankster.

'I hope you didn't take it without permission,' I said, taking the skull in my hands and admiring its symmetry but without philosophizing upon it like Hamlet.

'Oh, the college is full of them,' said Anil. 'I just borrowed it for the vacation.' He placed it on the mantelpiece, among some of the awards and mementos (cheap brassware mostly) that had accumulated over the years, and I must say it livened up the shelf a little.

Anil had placed the skull at one end of the mantelpiece, and there it stood until we'd had our dinner. He settled down with a book, while I poured myself a small glass of cognac before settling into an easy chair with a notebook on my knee. It was midsummer, and the window was open, so that we could hear the crickets singing in the oak trees. My cottage was on the outskirts of Mussoorie, surrounded by Himalayan oak and maple.

I had been making some notes for an article on wild flowers. When I had finished my notes and my cognac, I looked up and noticed that the skull now stood in the centre of the mantelpiece.

'Did you move the skull?' I asked.

'No,' said Anil, looking up. 'I placed it at the end of the shelf.'

'Well, it's now in the middle. How did it get there?'

'You must have moved it yourself, without noticing. That was a stiff cognac you drank, Uncle.'

I let it pass, it did not seem important.

◆

People often dropped in to see me. Schoolteachers, visitors to the hill station, students, other writers, neighbours. During that week I had a number of visitors, and of course everyone noticed the skull on the mantelpiece. Some were intrigued, and wanted to know whose skull it was. One or two lady teachers were frightened by it. A fellow writer thought it was in bad taste, displaying human remains in my sitting room. One visitor offered to buy it.

I would gladly have sold the wretched thing, but it belonged to Anil and he intended to take it back to Meerut. But when the time came to leave he forgot about the skull, his mind no doubt taken up with other matters—such as the daily phone calls he received from a girl student in Delhi. After seeing him off at the bus stop, I came home to find that the skull was still occupying pride of place on the mantelpiece.

I ignored it for a few days, and the skull didn't seem to mind that. It was receiving plenty of attention from visitors during the day.

But it was beginning to get on my nerves. Every evening, when I sat down to enjoy a whisky or a cognac, I would feel its empty eye sockets staring at me. And on one occasion, when I tried to change its position, my hand got caught in its jawbone and it was with some difficulty that I withdrew it.

Getting fed up of its presence, I decided to lock the thing

away where it wouldn't be seen.

There was a wall cupboard in the room, where I kept my manuscripts, notebooks, and writing materials, and there was plenty of space there for the skull. So I shifted it to the cupboard, and made sure the doors were locked.

That evening I enjoyed my drink without being watched by that remnant of a human head. The crickets were singing, a nightjar was calling, and a zephyr of a wind moved softly through the trees. I finished my article and went to bed in a happy frame of mind.

In the middle of the night I woke to a loud rattling sound. At first I thought it was a loose door latch or a wobbly drainpipe, then realized the noise was coming from the wall cupboard. A rat, perhaps? But no. As soon as I opened the cupboard door, out popped the skull, landing near my feet and bouncing away right across the drawing room.

For the sake of peace and quiet, I returned it to the mantelpiece. If a skull could smile, it would probably have done so. I went back to my bed and slept like a baby. It takes more than a dancing skull to keep me from enjoying a good night's sleep.

The next morning I got to work making up a parcel. Normally, I hate making parcels, they usually fall apart. But for once I took pleasure in making a parcel. I wrapped the skull in a plastic bag, then placed it in a strong cardboard box, wrapped this in brown parcel paper, used a liberal amount of Sellotape, and addressed the package to Dr Anil at his medical college. Then I walked into town and handed it over to the registration clerk at the post office.

Rubbing my hands with satisfaction, I treated myself to fish and chips and an ice cream before setting out on the walk down the hill to my cottage.

I was about halfway down the steep path that leads to one of our famous schools when I heard something rattling down the slope behind me. At first I thought it was an empty tin, but then I recognized my boon companion, that wretched skull, embellished with bits of wrapping paper and Sellotape, bouncing down the hill towards me. How did the skull get out of that parcel? I shall never know. Perhaps a nosy postal clerk had opened it to check the contents. I hope he got the fright of his life. I broke into a run, making a dash for the cottage door. But it was there before me, grinning up at me from a pot full of flowering petunias.

So back it went to its favourite place on the mantelpiece. And there it remained for several weeks.

◆

The school's playing field was situated just above the path to the cottage, and during the football season I could hear the boys kicking a football around.

One day a football escaped from the field and came bouncing down the hillside, landing on a flower bed. The match was over and no one bothered to come down to retrieve the ball. But it gave me an idea. I removed the bladder, stuffed the skull into the leather interior, and tied it up firmly. Then I had the football delivered to the school's games master, with my compliments.

Nothing happened for a couple of days. There was no shortage of footballs. Then in the middle of the game against St George's College, a ball went out of the grounds and a spare one was required.

The replacement did not bounce quite as well as the previous one, and it was inclined to spin around a lot and take off in directions opposite to those intended. Also, it squeaked whenever it received a kick, and sometimes those squeaks sounded a bit like screams of protest. The goalkeepers at either end found the ball difficult to hold, it did its best to elude their grasp. And more goals were scored by accident rather than design. Finally, this eccentric ball was kicked out of play and was replaced by another.

What happens to old footballs? I expect they finally fall apart and end up in a dustbin.

In this case, the football found a new owner, for the sports master was a kind man who gave away old bats, balls and other worn-out stuff to the poor children of the locality. A boy from a village near Rajpur was the recipient of the battered football, and he and his friends carried it away with a cheer, kicking it all the way down the steep path, making so much noise that they did not hear the groans of protest that issued from the battered old football.

Well, weeks passed, months passed, without the skull making a reappearance. But then something strange began to happen. I found myself missing that troublesome skull!

It had, after all, been company of a sort for a lonely writer living on his own on the edge of the forest. And when you have lived with someone for a long time, then, no matter how much you may quarrel or get on each other's nerves, a bond is formed, and the strength of that bond can only be known when it is broken.

The skull had been sharing my life for over a year, and now that it was gone, seemingly forever, my life seemed rather empty.

So I began searching for the skull. I enquired amongst the children down in Rajpur, but they had long since lost the football. I made a round of all the junk shops in Dehradun, without any luck. There were lots of old footballs lying around, but not the one I wanted. And, no, they didn't buy or sell human skulls.

Young Anil, the doctor, paid me a brief visit and found me

looking depressed.

'What's the trouble?' he asked. 'You look as though you've just lost a friend.'

'I have, indeed,' I said. 'I miss that skull you gave me. It was company of a sort.'

'Well, I'll get you another. No shortage of skulls in my college.'

'No, I don't want another. I want the same skull. It had a personality of its own.'

Anil looked at me as though he thought I was going off my rocker. And perhaps I was.

And then one day, as I was walking down a busy street in neighbouring Saharanpur, I noticed a fortune teller plying his trade on the pavement. I don't believe in fortune telling, but everyone has to make a living, and telling fortunes seems to me a harmless way of doing it. And then I noticed that he had a skull beside him, and that he would consult it before handing his customer a slip of paper with words of advice or encouragement written on it. It looked a bit like my skull, but I couldn't be sure. All the kicking and manhandling it had received had possibly altered its appearance.

But, anyway, I gave the fortune teller some money and asked him for a prediction. He chanted something, then extracted a slip of paper from beneath the skull and handed it to me with a flourish.

I read the words printed neatly on the paper.

'Ullu ka patha', went the message, followed by 'Gadhe ka baccha!'

It was definitely my skull! Only an old friend could abuse me like that.

So I pleaded and haggled with the fortune teller, paid him a hundred rupees for the skull, and carried it home in triumph.

And there it is today, decorating my mantelpiece, a little the worse for wear, and with a silly grin on its skeletal face. To improve its looks I have placed an old cricket cap on its head.

Sometimes we don't value our friends until we lose them.

EYES OF THE CAT

Ruskin Bond

Her eyes seemed flecked with gold when the sun was on them. And as the sun set over the mountains, drawing a deep red wound across the sky, there was more than gold in Binya's eyes. There was anger; for she had been cut to the quick by some remarks her teacher had made—the culmination of weeks of insults and taunts.

Binya was poorer than most of the girls in her class and could not afford the tuitions that had become almost obligatory if one was to pass and be promoted. 'You'll have to spend another year in the ninth,' said Madam. 'And if you don't like that, you can find another school—a school where it won't matter if your blouse is torn and your tunic is old and your shoes are falling apart.' Madam had shown her large teeth in what was supposed to be a good-natured smile, and all the girls had tittered dutifully. Sycophancy had become part of the curriculum in Madam's private academy for girls.

On the way home in the gathering gloom, Binya's two companions commiserated with her.

'She's a mean old thing,' said Usha. 'She doesn't care for anyone but herself.'

'Her laugh reminds me of a donkey braying,' said Sunita, who was more forthright.

But Binya wasn't really listening. Her eyes were fixed on some point in the far distance, where the pines stood in silhouette against a night sky that was growing brighter every moment. The moon was rising, a full moon, a moon that meant something very special to Binya, that made her blood tingle and her skin prickle and her hair glow and send out sparks. Her steps seemed to grow lighter, her limbs more sinewy as she moved gracefully, softly over the mountain path.

Abruptly she left her companions at a fork in the road.

'I'm taking the shortcut through the forest,' she said.

Her friends were used to her sudden whims. They knew she was not afraid of being alone in the dark. But Binya's moods made them feel a little nervous, and now, holding hands, they hurried home along the open road.

The shortcut took Binya through the dark oak forest. The crooked, tormented branches of the oaks threw twisted shadows across the path. A jackal howled at the moon; a nightjar called from urgency, and her breath came in short, sharp gasps. Bright moonlight bathed the hillside when she reached her home on the outskirts of the village.

Refusing her dinner, she went straight to her small room and flung the window open. Moonbeams crept over the window-sill and over her arms which were already covered with golden hair. Her strong nails had shredded the rotten wood of the window-sill.

Tail swishing and ears pricked, the tawny leopard came swiftly out of the window, crossed the open field behind the house, and melted into the shadows.

A little later it padded silently through the forest.

Although the moon shone brightly on the tin-roofed town, the leopard knew where the shadows were deepest and merged beautifully with them. An occasional intake of breath, which resulted in a short rasping cough, was the only sound it made.

Madam was returning from dinner at a ladies' club, called

the Kitten Club as a sort of foil to the husbands' club affiliations. There were still a few people in the street, and while no one could help noticing Madam, who had the contours of a steam-roller, none saw or heard the predator who had slipped down a side alley and reached the steps of the teacher's house. It sat there silently, waiting with all the patience of an obedient schoolgirl.

When Madam saw the leopard on her steps, she dropped her handbag and opened her mouth to scream; but her voice would not materialize. Nor would her tongue ever be used again, either to savour chicken biryani or to pour scorn upon her pupils, for the leopard had sprung at her throat, broken her neck, and dragged her into the bushes.

In the morning, when Usha and Sunita set out for school, they stopped as usual at Binya's cottage and called out to her.

Binya was sitting in the sun, combing her long black hair.

'Aren't you coming to school today, Binya?' asked the girls.

'No, I won't bother to go today,' said Binya. She felt lazy, but pleased with herself, like a contented cat.

'Madam won't be pleased,' said Usha. 'Shall we tell her you're sick?'

'It won't be necessary,' said Binya, and gave them one of her mysterious smiles. 'I'm sure it's going to be a holiday.'

THE EMPTY HOUSE

Algernon Blackwood

Certain houses, like certain persons, manage somehow to proclaim at once their character for evil. In the case of the latter, no particular feature need betray them; they may boast an open countenance and an ingenuous smile; and yet a little of their company leaves the unalterable conviction that there is something radically amiss with their being: that they are evil. Willy nilly) they seem to communicate an atmosphere of secret and wicked thoughts which makes those in their immediate neighbourhood shrink from them as from a thing diseased.

And, perhaps, with houses the same principle is operative, and it is the aroma of evil deeds committed under a particular roof, long after the actual doers have passed away, that makes the gooseflesh come and the hair rise. Something of the original passion of the evil-doer, and of the horror felt by his victim, enters the heart of the innocent watcher, and he becomes suddenly conscious of tingling nerves, creeping skin, and a chilling of the blood. He is terror-stricken without apparent cause.

There was manifestly nothing in the external appearance of this particular house to bear out the tales of the horror that was said to reign within. It was neither lonely nor unkempt. It stood, crowded into a corner of the square, and looked exactly like the houses on either side of it. It had the same number of windows as its neighbours; the same balcony overlooking the gardens; the same white steps leading up to the heavy black front door; and, in the rear, there was the same narrow strip of green, with neat box borders, running up to the wall that divided it from the backs of the adjoining houses. Apparently, too, the number of chimney pots on the roof was the same; the breadth and angle of the caves; and even the height of the dirty area railings.

And yet this house in the square, that seemed precisely similar to its fifty ugly neighbours, was as a matter of fact entirely different—horribly different.

Wherein lay this marked, invisible difference is impossible to say. It cannot be ascribed wholly to the imagination, because persons who had spent some time in the house, knowing nothing of the facts, had declared positively that certain rooms were so disagreeable they would rather die than enter them again, and that the atmosphere of the whole house produced in them symptoms of a genuine terror; while the series of innocent tenants who had tried to live in it and been forced to decamp at the shortest possible notice, was indeed little less than a scandal in the town.

When Shorthouse arrived to pay a 'weekend' visit to his Aunt Julia in her little house on the seafront at the other end of the town, he found her charged to the brim with mystery and excitement. He had only received her telegram that morning, and he had come anticipating boredom; but the moment he touched her hand and kissed her apple-skin wrinkled cheek, he caught the first waves of her electrical condition. The impression deepened when he learned that there were to be no other visitors, and that he had been telegraphed for with a very special object.

Something was in the wind, and the 'something' would doubtless bear fruit; for this elderly spinster aunt, with a mania for psychical research, had brains as well as will power, and by hook or by crook she usually managed to accomplish her ends. The revelation was made soon after tea, when she sidled close up to him as they paced slowly along the seafront in the dusk.

'I've got the keys,' she announced in a delighted, yet half awesome voice. 'Got them till Monday!'

'The keys of the bathing-machine, or—?' he asked innocently; looking from the sea to the town. Nothing brought her so quickly to the point as feigning stupidity.

'Neither,' she whispered. 'I've got the keys of the haunted house in the square—and I'm going there tonight.'

Shorthouse was conscious of the slightest possible tremor down his back. He dropped his teasing tone. Something in her voice and manner thrilled him. She was in earnest.

'But you can't go alone—' he began.

'That's why I wired for you,' she said with decision.

He turned to look at her. The ugly, lined, enigmatical face was alive with excitement. There was the glow of genuine enthusiasm round it like a halo. The eyes shone. He caught another wave of her excitement, and a second tremor, more marked than the first, accompanied it.

'Thanks, Aunt Julia,' he said politely; 'thanks awfully.'

'I should not dare to go quite alone,' she went on, raising her voice; 'But with you I should enjoy it immensely You're afraid of nothing, I know.'

'Thanks so much,' he said again. 'Er—is anything likely to happen?'

'A great deal *has* happened,' she whispered, 'though it's been most cleverly hushed up. Three tenants have come and ,one in the last few months, and the house is said to be empty for good now.'

In spite of himself, Shorthouse became interested. His aunt

was so very much in earnest.

'The house is very old indeed,' she went on, 'and the story—an unpleasant one—dates a long way back. It has to do with a murder committed by a jealous stableman who had some affair with a servant in the house. One night he managed to secrete himself in the cellar, and when everyone was asleep, he crept upstairs to the servants' quarters, chased the girl down to the next landing, and before anyone could come to the rescue threw her bodily over the bannisters into the hall below.'

'And the stableman—?'

'Was caught, I believe, and hanged for murder; but it all happened a century ago, and I've not been able to get more details of the story.'

Shorthouse now felt his interest thoroughly aroused but, though he was not particularly nervous for himself, he hesitated a little on his aunt's account.

'On one condition,' he said at length.

'Nothing will prevent my going,' she said firmly; 'but I may as well hear your condition.'

'That you guarantee your power of self-control if anything really horrible happens. I mean—that you are sure you won't get too frightened.'

'Jim,' she said scornfully, 'I'm not young, I know, nor are my nerves; but *with you* I should be afraid of nothing in the world!'

This, of course, settled it, for Shorthouse had no pretensions to being other than a very ordinary young man, and an appeal to his vanity was irresistible. He agreed to go.

Instinctively; by a sort of subconscious preparation, he kept himself and his forces well in hand the whole evening, compelling an accumulative reserve of control by that nameless inward process of gradually putting all the emotions away and turning the key upon them—a process difficult to describe, but wonderfully effective, as all men who have lived through severe trials of the inner man well understand. Later, it stood him in good stead.

But it was not until half past ten, when they stood in the hall, well in the glare of friendly lamps and still surrounded by comforting human influences, that he had to make the first call upon this store of collected strength. For, once the door was closed, and he saw the deserted silent street stretching away white in the moonlight before them, it came to him clearly that the real test that night would be in dealing with *two fears* instead of one. He would have to carry his aunt's fear as well as his own. And, as he glanced down at her sphinx-like countenance and realized that it might assume no pleasant aspect in a rush of real terror, he felt satisfied with only one thing in the whole adventure—that he had confidence in his own will and power to stand against any shock that might come.

Slowly they walked along the empty streets of the town; a bright autumn moon silvered the roofs, casting deep shadows; there was no breath of wind; and the trees in the formal gardens by the seafront watched them silently as they passed along. To his aunt's occasional remarks Shorthouse made no reply; realizing that she was simply surrounding herself with mental buffers—saying ordinary things to prevent herself thinking of extraordinary things. Few windows showed lights, and from scarcely a single chimney came smoke or sparks. Shorthouse had already begun to notice everything, even the smallest details. Presently they stopped at the street corner and looked up at the name on the side of the house full in the moonlight, and with one accord, but without remark, turned into the square and crossed over to the side of it that lay in shadow.

'The number of the house is thirteen,' whispered a voice at his side; and neither of them made the obvious reference, but passed across the broad sheet of moonlight and began to march up the pavement in silence.

It was about half-way up the square that Shorthouse felt an arm slipped quietly but significantly into his own, and knew then that their adventure had begun in earnest, and that his companion was already yielding imperceptibly to the influences against them. She needed support.

A few minutes later they stopped before a tall, narrow house that rose before them into the night, ugly in shape and painted a dingy white. Shutterless windows, without blinds, stared down upon them, shining here and there in the moonlight. There were weather streaks in the wall and cracks in the paint, and the balcony bulged out from the first floor a little unnaturally. But, beyond this generally forlorn appearance of an unoccupied house, there was nothing at first sight to single out this particular mansion for the evil character it had most certainly acquired.

Taking a look over their shoulders to make sure they had not been followed, they went boldly up the steps and stood against the huge black door that fronted them forbiddingly. But the first wave of nervousness was now upon them, and Shorthouse fumbled a long time with the key before he could fit it into the lock at all. For a moment, if truth were told, they both hoped it would not open, for they were a prey to various unpleasant emotions as they stood there on the threshold of their ghostly adventure. Shorthouse, shuffling with the key and hampered by the steady weight on his arm, certainly felt the solemnity of the moment. It was as if the whole world—for all experience seemed at that instant concentrated in his own consciousness—were listening to the grating noise of that key. A stray puff of wind wandering down the empty street woke a momentary rustling in the trees behind them, but otherwise this rattling of the key was the only sound audible; and at last it turned in the lock and the heavy door swung open and revealed a yawning gulf of darkness beyond.

With a last glance at the moonlit square, they passed quickly in, and the door slammed behind them with a roar that echoed prodigiously through empty halls and passages. But, instantly, with the echoes, another sound made itself heard, and Aunt Julia leaned suddenly so heavily upon him that he had to take a step backwards to save himself from falling.

A man had coughed close beside them—so close that it seethed they must have been actually by his side in the darkness.

With the possibility of practical jokes in his mind, Shorthouse at once swung his heavy stick in the direction of the sound; but it met nothing more solid than air. He heard his aunt give a little gasp beside him.

'There's someone here,' she whispered: 'I heard him.'

'Be quiet!' he said sternly. 'It was nothing but the noise of the front door.'

'Oh! Get a light—quick!' she added, as her nephew fumbling with a box of matches, opened it upside down and let them all fall with a rattle on to the stone floor.

The sound, however, was not repeated; and there was no evidence of retreating footsteps. In another minute they had a candle burning, using an empty end of a cigar case as a holder; and when the first flare had died down he held the impromptu lamp aloft and surveyed the scene. And it was dreary enough in all conscience, for there is nothing more desolate in all the abodes of men than an unfurnished house dimly lit, silent, and forsaken, and yet tenanted by rumour with the memories of evil and violent histories.

They were standing in a wide hallway; on their left was the open door of a spacious dining room, and in front the hall ran, ever narrowing, into a long, dark passage that led apparently to the top of the kitchen stairs. The broad uncarpeted staircase rose in a sweep before them, everywhere draped in shadows, except for a single spot about half-way up where the moonlight came in through the window and fell on a bright patch on the boards. This shaft of light shed a faint radiance above and below it, lending to the objects within its reach a misty outline that was infinitely more suggestive and ghostly than complete darkness. Filtered moonlight always seems to paint faces on the surrounding gloom, and as Shorthouse peered up into the well of darkness and thought of the countless empty rooms and passages in the upper part of the old house, he caught himself longing again for the safety of the moonlit square, or the cosy, bright drawing-room they had left an hour before. Then realizing that these thoughts were dangerous, he thrust them away again and summoned all his energy for concentration on the present.

'Aunt Julia,' he said aloud, severer; 'we must now go through the house from top to bottom and make a thorough search.'

The echoes of his voice died away slowly all over the building, and in the intense silence that followed he turned to look at her. In the candlelight he saw that her face was already ghastly pale; but she dropped his arm for a moment and said in a whisper, stepping close in front of him—

'I agree. We must be sure there's no one hiding. That's the first thing.'

She spoke with evident effort, and he looked at her with admiration.

'You feel quite sure of yourself? It's not too late—'

'I think so,' she whispered, her eyes shifting nervously toward the shadows behind. 'Quite sure, only one thing—'

'What's that?'

'You must never leave me alone for an instant.'

'As long as you understand that any sound or appearance

must be investigated at once, for to hesitate means to admit fear. That is fatal.'

'Agreed,' she said, a little shakily; after a moment's hesitation. 'I'll try—'

Arm in arm, Shorthouse holding the dripping candle and the stick, while his aunt carried the cloak over her shoulders, figures of utter comedy to all but themselves, they began a systematic search. Stealthily, walking on tiptoe and shading the candle lest it should betray their presence through the shutterless windows, they went first into the big dining room. There was not a stick of furniture to be seen. Bare walls, ugly mantelpieces and empty grates stared at them. Everything, they felt, resented their intrusion, watching them, as it were, with veiled eyes; whispers followed them; shadows flitted noiselessly to right and left; something seemed ever at their back, watching, waiting an opportunity to do them injury. There was the inevitable sense that operations which went on when the room was empty had been temporarily suspended till they were well out of the way again. The whole dark interior of the old building seemed to become a malignant Presence that rose tip, warning them to desist and mind their own business; every moment the strain on the nerves increased.

Out of the gloomy dining room they passed through large folding doors into a sort of library or smoking room, wrapt equally in silence, darkness, and dust; and from this they regained the hall near the top of the back stairs.

Here a pitch black tunnel opened before them into the lower regions, and—it must be confessed—they hesitated. But only for a minute. With the worst of the night still to come it was essential to turn from nothing. Aunt Julia stumbled at the top step of the dark descent, ill-lit by the flickering candle, and even Shorthouse felt at least half the decision go out of his legs.

'Come on!' he said peremptorily, and his voice ran on and lost itself in the dark, empty spaces below.

'I'm coming,' she faltered, catching his arm with unnecessary violence.

They went a little unsteadily down the stone steps, a cold, damp air meeting them in the face, close and malodorous. The kitchen, into which the stairs led along a narrow passage, was large, with a lofty ceiling. Several doors opened out of it—some into cupboards with empty jars still standing on the shelves, and others into horrible little ghostly back offices, each colder and less inviting than the last. Black beetles scurried over the floor, and once, when they knocked against a deal table standing in a corner, something about the size of a cat jumped down with a rush and fled, scampering across the stone floor into the darkness. Everywhere there was a sense of recent occupation, an impression of sadness and gloom.

Leaving the plain kitchen, they next went towards the scullery. The door was standing ajar, and as they pushed it open to its full extent Aunt Julia uttered a piercing scream, which she instantly tried to stifle by placing her hand over her mouth. For a second Shorthouse stood stock-still, catching his breath. He felt as if his spine had suddenly become hollow and someone had filled it with particles of ice.

Facing them, directly in their way between the doorposts, stood the figure of a woman. She had dishevelled hair and wildly staring eyes, and her face was terrified and white as death.

She stood there motionless for the space of a single second. Then the candle flickered and she was gone—gone utterly—and the door framed nothing but empty darkness.

'Only the beastly jumping candlelight,' he said quickly, in a voice that sounded like someone else's and was only half under control. 'Come on, aunt. There's nothing there.'

He dragged her forward. With a clattering of feet and a great appearance of boldness they went on, but over his body the skin moved as if crawling ants covered it, and he knew by the weight on his arm that he was supplying the force of locomotion for two. The scullery was cold, bare, and empty; more like a large prison cell than anything else. They went round it, tried the door into the yard, and the windows, but found them all fastened securely. His aunt moved beside him like a person in a dream. Her eyes were tightly shut, and she seemed merely to follow the pressure of his arm. Her courage filled him with amazement. At the same time he noticed that a certain odd change had come over her face, a change which somehow evaded his power of analysis.

'There's nothing here, aunty,' he repeated aloud quickly 'Let's go upstairs and see the rest of the house. Then we'll choose a room to wait up in.'

She followed him obediently keeping close to his side, and they locked the kitchen door behind them. It was a relief to get up again. In the hall there was more light than before, for the moon had travelled a little further down the stairs. Cautiously they began to go up into the dark vault of the upper house, the boards creaking under their weight.

On the first floor they found the large double drawing rooms, a search of which revealed nothing. Here also was no sign of furniture or recent occupancy; nothing but dust and neglect and shadows. They opened the big folding doors between front and back drawing rooms and then came out again to the landing and went on upstairs.

They had not gone up more than a dozen steps when they both simultaneously stopped to listen, looking into each other's eyes with a new apprehension across the flickering candle flame. From the room they had left hardly ten seconds before came the sound of doors quietly closing. It was beyond all question; they heard the booming noise that accompanies the shutting of heavy doors, followed by the sharp catching of the latch.

'We must go back and see,' said Shorthouse briefly, in a low tone, and turning to go downstairs again.

Somehow she managed to drag after him, her feet catching in her dress, her face livid.

When they entered the front drawing rooms it was plain that the folding doors had been closed—half a minute before. Without hesitation Shorthouse opened them. He almost expected to see someone facing him in the back room; but only darkness and cold air met him. They went through both rooms, finding nothing unusual. They tried in every way to make the doors close of themselves, but there was not wind enough even to set the candle flame flickering. The doors would not move without strong pressure. All was silent as the grave. Undeniably the rooms were utterly empty; and the house utterly still.

'It's beginning.' Whispered a voice at his elbow which he hardly recognized as his aunt's.

He nodded acquiescence, taking out his watch to note the time. It was fifteen minutes before midnight; he made the entry of exactly what had occurred in his notebook, setting the candle in its case upon the floor in order to do so. It took a moment or two to balance it safely against the wall.

Aunt Julia always declared that at this moment she was not actually watching him, but had turned her head towards the inner room, where she fancied she heard something moving; but, at any rate, both positively agreed that there came a sound of rushing feet, heavy and very swift—and the next instant the candle was out!

But to Shorthouse himself had come more than this, and he has always thanked his fortunate stars that it came to him alone and not to his aunt too. For, as he rose from the stooping position of balancing the candle, and before it was actually extinguished, a face thrust itself forward so close to his own that he could almost have touched it with his lips. It was a face working with passion; a man's face, dark, with thick features, and angry, savage eyes. It belonged to a common man, and it was evil in its ordinary normal expression, no doubt, but as he saw it, alive with intense, aggressive emotion it was a malignant and terrible human countenance.

There was no movement of the air; nothing but the sound of rushing feet—stockinged or muffled feet; the apparition of the face; and the almost simultaneous extinguishing of the candle.

In spite of himself, Shorthouse uttered a little cry, nearly losing his balance as his aunt clung to him with her whole weight in one moment of real, uncontrollable terror. She made no sound, but simply seized him bodily. Fortunately, however, she had seen nothing, but had only heard the rushing feet, for her control returned almost at once, and he was able to disentangle himself and strike a match.

The shadows ran away on all sides before the glare, and his aunt stooped down and groped for the cigar case with the precious candle. Then they discovered that the candle had not been blown out at all; it had been *crushed* out. The wick was pressed down into the wax, which was flattened as if by some smooth, heavy instrument.

How his companion so quickly overcame her terror, Shorthouse never properly understood; but his admiration for her self-control increased tenfold, and at the same time served to feed his own dying flame—for which he was undeniably grateful. Equally inexplicable to him was the evidence of physical force they had just witnessed. He at once suppressed the memory of stories he had heard of 'physical mediums' and their dangerous phenomena; for if these were true, and either his aunt or himself was unwittingly a physical medium, it meant that they were simply aiding to focus the forces of a haunted house already charged to the brim. It was like walking with unprotected lamps among uncovered stores of gunpowder.

So, with as little reflection as possible, he simply relit the candle and went up to the next floor. The arm in his trembled, it is true, and his own tread was often uncertain, but they went on with thoroughness, and after a search revealing nothing they climbed the last flight of stairs to the top floor of all.

Here they found a perfect nest of small servants' rooms, with broken pieces of furniture, dirty cane-bottomed chairs, chests of drawers, cracked mirrors, and decrepit bedsteads. The rooms had low sloping ceilings already hung here and there with cobwebs, small windows, and badly plastered walls—a depressing and dismal region which they were glad to leave behind.

It was on the stroke of midnight when they entered a small room on the third floor, close to the top of the stairs, and arranged to make themselves comfortable for the remainder of their adventure. It was absolutely bare, and was said to be the room—then used as a clothes closet—into which the infuriated groom had chased his victim and finally caught her. Outside, across the narrow landing, began the stairs leading up to the floor above, and the servants' quarters where they had just searched.

In spite of the chilliness of the night there was something in the air of this room that cried for an open window. But there was more than this. Shorthouse could only describe it by saying that he felt less master of himself here than in any other part of the house. There was something that acted directly on the nerves, tiring the resolution, enfeebling the will. He was conscious of this result before he had been in the room five minutes, and it was in the short time they stayed there that he suffered the wholesale depletion of his vital forces, which was, for himself, the chief horror of the whole experience.

They put the candle on the floor of the cupboard, leaving the door a few inches ajar, so that there was no glare to confuse the eyes, and no shadow to shift about on walls and ceiling. Then they spread the cloak on the floor and sat down to wait, with their backs against the wall.

Shorthouse was within two feet of the door on to the landing; his position commanded a good view of the main staircase leading down into the darkness, and also of the beginning of, the servants' stairs going to the floor above; the heavy stick lay beside him within easy reach.

The moon was now high above the house. Through the open window they could see the comforting stars like friendly eyes watching in the sky. One by one the clocks of the town struck midnight, and when the sounds died away the deep silence of a windless night fell again over everything. Only the boom of the sea, far away and lugubrious, filled the air with hollow murmurs.

Inside the house the silence became awful; awful, he thought, because any minute now it might be broken by sounds portending terror. The strain of waiting told more and more severely on the nerves; they talked in whispers when they talked at all, for their voices aloud sounded queer and unnatural. A chilliness, not altogether due to the night air, invaded the room, and made them cold. The influences against them, whatever these might be, were slowly robbing them of self-confidence, and the power of decisive action: their forces were on the wane, and the possibility of real fear took on a new and terrible meaning. He began to tremble for the elderly woman by his side, whose pluck could hardly save her beyond a certain extent.

He heard the blood singing in his veins. It sometimes seemed so loud that he fancied it prevented his hearing properly certain other sounds that were beginning very faintly to make themselves audible in the depths of the house. Every time he fastened his attention on these sounds, they instantly ceased. They certainly came no nearer. Yet he could not rid himself of the idea that movement was going on somewhere in the lower regions of the house. The drawing rooms floor, where the door had been so strangely closed, seemed too near; the sounds were further off than that. He thought of the great kitchen, with the scurrying black beetles, and of the dismal little scullery; but, somehow or other, they did not seem to come from there either. Surely they were not *outside* the house!

Then, suddenly, the truth flashed into his mind, and for the space of a minute he felt as if his blood had stopped flowing and turned to ice.

The sounds were not downstairs at all; they were *upstairs*—upstairs, somewhere among those horrid gloomy little servants' rooms with their bits of broken furniture, low ceilings, and cramped windows—upstairs where the victim had first been disturbed and stalked to her death.

And the moment he discovered where the sounds were, he began to hear them more clearly. It was the sound of feet, moving stealthily along the passage overhead, in and out among the rooms, and past the furniture.

He turned quickly to steal a glance at the motionless figure seated beside him, to note whether she had shared his discovery The faint candlelight coming through the crack in the cupboard door, threw her strongly-marked face into vivid relief against the white of the wall. But it was something else that made him catch his breath and stare again. An extraordinary something had come into her face and seemed to spread over her features like a mask; it smoothed out the deep lines and drew the skin everywhere a little tighter so that the wrinkles disappeared; it brought into the face—with the sole exception of the old eyes—an appearance of youth and almost of childhood.

He stared in speechless amazement—amazement that was dangerously near to horror. It was his aunt's face indeed, but it was her face of forty years ago, the vacant innocent face of a girl. He had heard stories of that strange effect of terror which could wipe a human countenance clean of other emotions, obliterating all previous expression; but he had never realized that it could be literally true, or could mean anything so simply horrible as what he now saw for the dreadful signature of overmastering fear was written plainly in that utter vacancy of the girlish face beside him; and when, feeling his intense gaze, she turned to look at him, he instinctively closed his eves tightly to shut out the sight.

Yet, when he turned a minute later, his feelings well in hand, he saw to his intense relief another expression; his aunt was smiling, and though the face was deathly white, the awful veil had lifted and the normal look was returning.

'Anything wrong?' was all he could think of to say at the moment. And the answer was eloquent, coming from such a woman.

'I feel cold—and a little frightened,' she whispered.

He offered to close the window, but she seized hold of him and begged him not to leave her side even for an instant.

'It's upstairs, I know,' she whispered, with an odd half laugh; 'but I can't possibly go up.'

But Shorthouse thought otherwise, knowing that in action lay their best hope of self-control.

He took the brandy flash and poured out a glass of neat spirit, stiff enough to help anybody over anything. She swallowed it with a little shiver. His only idea now was to get out of the house before her collapse became inevitable; but this could not safely be done by turning tail and running from the enemy. Inaction was no longer possible; every minute he was growing less master of himself, and desperate, aggressive measures were imperative without further delay. Moreover, the action must be taken *towards* the enemy; not away from it; the climax, if necessary and unavoidable, would have to be faced boldly. He could do it now; but in ten minutes he might not have the force left to act for himself, much less for both!

Upstairs, the sounds were meanwhile becoming louder and closer, accompanied by occasional creaking of the boards. Someone was moving stealthily about, stumbling now and then awkwardly against the furniture.

Waiting a few moments to allow the tremendous dose of spirits to produce its effect, and knowing this would last but a short time under the circumstances, Shorthouse then quietly got on his feet, saying in a determined voice—

'Now, Aunt Julia, we'll go upstairs and find out what all this noise is about. You must come too. It's what we agreed.'

He picked tip his stick and went to the cupboard for the candle. A limp form rose shakily beside him breathing hard, and he heard a voice say very faintly something about being 'ready to come'. The woman's courage amazed him; it was so much greater than his own: and, as they advanced, holding aloft the dripping candle, some subtle force exhaled from this trembling, white-faced old woman at his side that was the true source of his inspiration. It held something really great that shamed him and gave him the support without which he would have proved far less equal to the occasion.

They crossed the dark landing, avoiding with their eyes the deep black space over the banisters. Then they began to mount the narrow staircase to meet the sounds which, minute by minute, grew louder and nearer. About half-way up the stairs Aunt Julia stumbled and Shorthouse turned to catch her by the arm, and just at that moment there came a terrific crash in the servants' corridor overhead. It was instantly followed by a shrill, agonized scream that was a cry of terror and a cry for help melted into one.

Before they could move aside, or go down a single step, someone came rushing along the passage overhead, blundering horribly, racing madly, at full speed, three steps at a time, down the very staircase where they stood. The steps were light and uncertain; but close behind them sounded the heavier tread of another person, and the staircase seemed to shake.

Shorthouse and his companion just had time to flatten themselves against the wall when the jumble of flying steps was upon them, and two persons, with the slightest possible interval between them, dashed past at full speed. It was a perfect whirlwind of sound breaking in upon the midnight silence of the empty building.

The two runners, pursuer and pursued, had passed clean through them where they stood, and already with a thud the boards below had received first one, then the other. Yet they had seen absolutely nothing—not a hand, or arm, or face, or even a shred of flying clothing.

There came a second's pause. Then the first one, the lighter of the two, obviously the pursued one, ran with uncertain footsteps into the little room which Shorthouse and his aunt had just left. The heavier one followed. There was a sound of scuffling, gasping, and smothered screaming; and then out on to the landing came the step—of a single person *treading weightily.*

A dead silence followed for the space of half a minute, and then was heard a rushing sound through the air. It was followed by a dull, crashing thud in the depths of the house below—on the stone floor of the hall.

Utter silence reigned after. Nothing moved. The flame of the candle was steady. It had been steady the whole time, and the air had been undisturbed by any movement whatsoever. Palsied with terror, Aunt Julia, without waiting for her companion, began fumbling her way downstairs; she was crying gently to herself, and when Shorthouse put his arm round her and half carried her he felt that she was trembling like a leaf. He went into the little room and picked up the cloak from the floor, and, arm in arm, walking very slowly, without speaking a word or looking once behind them, they marched down the three flights into the hall.

In the hall they saw nothing, but the whole way down the stairs they were conscious that someone followed them; step by step; when they went faster IT was left behind, and when they went more slowly IT caught them up. But never once did they look behind to see; and at each turning of the staircase they lowered their eyes for fear of the following horror they might see upon the stairs above.

With trembling hands Shorthouse opened the front door, and they walked out into the moonlight and drew a deep breath of the cool night air blowing in from the sea.

THE PERFECT MURDER

Stacy Aumonier

One evening in November two brothers were seated in a little café in the Rue de la Roquette discussing murders. The evening papers lay in front of them, and they all contained a lurid account of a shocking affair in the Landes district, where a charcoal-burner had killed his wife and two children with a hatchet. From discussing this murder in particular they went on to discussing murder in general.

'I've never yet read a murder case without being impressed by the extraordinary clumsiness of it,' remarked Paul, the younger brother. 'Here's this fellow who murders his victims with his own hatchet, leaves his hat behind in the shed, and arrives at a village hard by with blood on his boots.'

'They lose their heads,' said Henri, the elder. 'In cases like that they are mentally unbalanced, hardly responsible for their actions.'

'Yes,' replied Paul, 'but what impresses me is—what a lot of murders must be done by people who take trouble, who leave not a trace behind.'

Henri shrugged his shoulders. 'I shouldn't think it was so easy, old boy; there's always something that crops up.'

'Nonsense! I'll guarantee there are thousands done every year. If you are living with anyone, for instance, it must be the easiest thing in the world to murder them.'

'How?'

'Oh, some kind of accident—and then you go screaming into the street, "Oh, my poor wife! Help!" You burst into tears, and everyone consoles you. I read of a woman somewhere who murdered her husband by leaving the window near the bed open at night when he was suffering from pneumonia. Who's going to suspect a case like that? Instead of that, people must always select revolvers, or knives, or go and buy poison at the chemist's across the way.'

'It sounds as though you were contemplating a murder yourself,' laughed Henri.

'Well, you never know,' answered Paul; 'circumstances might arise when a murder would be the only way out of a difficulty. If ever my time comes I shall take a lot of trouble about it. I promise you I shall leave no trace behind.'

As Henri glanced at his brother making this remark he was struck by the fact that there was indeed nothing irreconcilable between the idea of a murder and the idea of Paul doing it. He was a big, saturnine-looking gentleman with a sallow, dissolute face, framed in a black square beard and swathes of untidy grey hair. His profession was that of a traveller in cheap jewellery, and his business dealings were not always of the straightest. Henri shuddered. With his own puny physique, bad health, and vacillating will, he was always dominated by his younger brother. He himself was a clerk in a drapery store, and he had a wife and three children. Paul was unmarried.

The brothers saw a good deal of each other, and were very intimate. But the word friendship would be an extravagant term to apply to their relationship. They were both always hard up, and they borrowed money from each other when every other source failed.

They had no other relatives except a very old uncle and aunt who lived at Chantilly. This uncle and aunt, whose name was Taillandier, were fairly well off, but they would have little to do with the two nephews. They were occasionally invited there to dinner, but neither Paul nor Henri ever succeeded in extracting a franc out of Uncle Robert. He was a very religious man, hard-fisted, cantankerous, and intolerant. His wife was a little more pliable. She was in effect an eccentric. She had spasms of generosity, during which periods both the brothers had at times managed to get money out of her. But these were rare occasions. Moreover, the old man kept her so short of cash that she found it difficult to help her nephews even if she desired to.

As stated, the discussion between the two brothers occurred in November. It was presumably forgotten by both of them immediately afterwards. And indeed, there is no reason to believe that it would ever have recurred, except for certain events which followed the sudden death of Uncle Robert in the February of the following year.

In the meantime, the affairs of both Paul and Henri had gone disastrously. Paul had been detected in a dishonest transaction over a paste trinket, and had just been released from a period of imprisonment. The knowledge of this had not reached his uncle before his death. Henri's wife had had another baby, and had been very ill. He was more in debt than ever.

The news of the uncle's death came as a glean of hope in the darkness of despair. What kind of will had he left? Knowing their uncle, each was convinced that, however it was framed there was likely to be little or nothing for them. However, the old villain might have left them a thousand or two. And in any case, if the money was all left to the wife, here was a possible field of plunder. It need hardly be said that they repaired with all haste to the funeral, and even with greater alacrity to the lawyer's reading of the will.

The will contained surprises both encouraging and

discouraging. In the first place the old man left a considerably larger fortune than anyone could have anticipated. In the second place all the money and securities were carefully tied up, and placed under the control of trustees. There were large bequests to religious charities, whilst the residue was held in trust for his wife. But so far as the brothers were concerned the surprise came at the end. On her death this residue was still to be held in trust, but a portion of the interest was to be divided between Henri and Paul, and on their death to go to the Church. The old man had recognized a certain call of the blood after all!

They both behaved with tact and discretion at the funeral, and were extremely sympathetic and solicitous towards Aunt Rosalie, who was too absorbed with her own trouble to take much notice of them. It was only when it came to the reading of the will that their avidity and interest outraged perhaps the strict canons of good taste. It was Paul who managed to get it clear from the notary what the exact amount would probably be. Making allowances for fluctuations, accidents, and acts of God, on the death of Mme Taillandier the two brothers would inherit something between eight and ten thousand francs a year each. She was eighty-two and very frail.

The brothers celebrated the good news with a carouse up in Montmartre. Naturally their chief topic of conversation was how long the old bird would keen on her perch. In any case, it could not be many years. With any luck it might be only a few weeks. The fortune seemed blinding. It would mean comfort and security to the end of their days. The rejoicings were mixed with recriminations against the old man for his stinginess. Why couldn't he have left them a lump sum down now? Why did he want to waste all this good gold on the Church? Why all this trustee business?

There was little they could do but await developments.

Except that in the meantime—after a decent interval—they might try and touch the old lady for a bit. They parted, and the next day set about their business in cheerier spirits.

For a time they were extremely tactful. They made formal calls on Aunt Rosalie, inquiring after her health, and offering their services in any capacity whatsoever. But at the end of a month Henri called hurriedly one morning, and after the usual professions of solicitude asked his aunt if she could possibly lend him one hundred and twenty francs to pay the doctor who had attended his wife and baby. She lent him forty, grumbling at his foolishness at having children he could not afford to keep. A week later came Paul with a story about being robbed by a client. He wanted a hundred. She lent him ten.

When these appeals had been repeated three or four times, and received similar treatment—and sometimes no treatment at all—the old lady began to get annoyed. She was becoming more and more eccentric. She now had a companion, an angular, middle-aged woman named Mme Chavanne, who appeared like a protecting goddess. Sometimes when the brothers called, Mme Chavanne would say that Mme Taillandier was too unwell to see anyone. If this news had been true it would have been good news indeed, but the brothers suspected that it was all pre-arranged. Two years went by, and they both began to despair.

'She may live to a hundred,' said Paul.

'We shall die of old age, first,' grumbled Henri.

It was difficult to borrow money on the strength of the will. In the first place their friends were more of the borrowing than the lending class. And, anyone who had a little was suspicious of the story, and wanted all kinds of securities. It was Paul who first thought of going to an insurance company to try to raise money on the reversionary interest. They did succeed in the end in getting an insurance company to advance them two thousand francs each, but the negotiations took five months to complete, and by the time they had insured their lives, paid the lawyer's fees and paid for the various deeds and stamps, and signed some thirty or forty forms, each man only received a little over a thousand francs, which was quickly lost in paying accrued debts and squandering the remainder. Their hopes were raised by the dismissal of Mme Chavanne, only to be lowered again by the arrival of an even more aggressive companion. The companions came and went with startling rapidity. None of them could stand for any time the old lady's eccentricity and ill-temper. The whole of the staff was always being changed. The only one who remained loyal all through was the portly cook, Ernestine. Even this may have been due to the fact that she never came in touch with her mistress. She was an excellent cook, and she never moved from the kitchen. Moreover, the cooking required by Mme Taillandier was of the simplest nature, and she seldom entertained. And, she hardly ever left her apartment. Any complaints that were made were made through the housekeeper, and the complaints and their retaliations became mellowed in the process; for Ernestine also had a temper of her own.

Nearly another year passed before what appeared to Paul to be a mild stroke of good fortune came his way. Things had been going from bad to worse. Neither of the brothers was in a position to lend a sou to the other. Henri's family was becoming a greater drag, and people were not buying Paul's trinkets.

One day, during an interview with his aunt—he had been trying to borrow more money—he fainted in her presence. It is difficult to know what it was about this act which affected the old lady, but she ordered him to be put to bed in one of the rooms of the villa. Possibly, she jumped to the conclusion that he had fainted from lack of food—which was not true, Paul never went without food and drink—and she suddenly realized that after all he was her husband's sister's son. He must certainly have looked pathetic, this white-faced man, well past middle age, and broken in life. Whatever it was, she showed a broad streak of compassion for him. She ordered her servants to look after him, and to allow him to remain until she countermanded the order.

Paul, who had certainly felt faint, but quickly seized the occasion to make it as dramatic as possible, saw in this an opportunity to wheedle his way into his aunt's favours. His behaviour was exemplary. The next morning, looking very white and shaky, he visited her, and asked her to allow him to go, as he had no idea of abusing her hospitality. If he had taken up the opposite attitude she would probably have turned him out, but because he suggested going she ordered him to stop. During the daytime he went about his dubious business, but he continued to return there at night to sleep, and to enjoy a good dinner cooked by the admirable Ernestine. He was in clover.

Henri was naturally envious when he heard of his brother's good fortune. And, Paul was fearful that Henri would spoil the whole game by going and throwing a fit himself in the presence of the aunt. But this, of course, would have been too obvious and foolish for even Henri to consider seriously. And, he racked his brains for some means of inveigling the old lady. Every plan he put forth, however, Paul sat upon. He was quite comfortable himself, and he didn't see the point of his brother butting in.

'Besides,' he said, 'she may turn me out any day. Then you can have your shot.'

They quarrelled about this, and did not see each other for some time. One would have thought that Henri's appeal to Mme Taillandier would have been stronger than Paul's. He was a struggling individual, with a wife and four children. Paul was a notorious ne'er-do-well, and he had no attachments.

Nevertheless, the old lady continued to support Paul. Perhaps, it was because he was a big man, and she liked big men. Her husband had been a man of fine physique. Henri was puny, and she despised him. She had never had children of her own, and she disliked children. She was always upbraiding Henri and his wife for their fecundity. Any attempt to pander to her emotions through the sentiment of childhood failed. She would not have the children in her house. And, any small acts of charity which she bestowed upon them seemed to be done more with the idea of giving her an opportunity to inflict her sarcasm and venom upon them than out of kindness of heart.

In Paul, on the other hand, she seemed to find something slightly attractive. She sometimes sent for him, and he, all agog—expecting to get his notice to quit—would be agreeably surprised to find that, on the contrary, she had some little commission she wished him to execute. And, you may rest assured that he never failed to make a few francs out of all these occasions. The notice to quit did not come. It may be—poor deluded woman—that she regarded him as some kind of protection. He was in any case the only 'man' who slept under her roof.

At first she seldom spoke to him, but as time went on she would sometimes send for him to relieve her loneliness. Nothing could have been more ingratiating than Paul's manners in these knowing circumstances. He talked expansively about politics, beforehand his aunt's views, and just what she would like him to say. Her eyesight was very bad, and he would read her the news of the day, and tell her what was happening in Paris. He humoured her every whim. He was astute enough to see that it would be foolish and dangerous to attempt to borrow money for the moment. He was biding his time, and trying to think out the most profitable plan of campaign. There was no immediate hurry. His bed was comfortable, and Ernestine's cooking was excellent.

In another year's time he had established himself as quite one of the permanent household. He was consulted about the servants, and the doctors, and the management of the house, everything except the control of money, which was jealously guarded by a firm of lawyers. Many a time he would curse his uncle's foresight. The old man's spirit seemed to be hovering in the dim recesses of the over-crowded rooms, mocking him. For the old lady, eccentric and foolish in many ways, kept a strict check upon her dividends. It was her absorbing interest in life, that and an old grey perroquet, which she treated like a child. Its name was Anna, and it used to walk up and down her table at mealtimes and feed off her own plate. Finding himself so firmly entrenched Paul's assurance gradually increased. He began to treat his aunt as an equal, and sometimes even to contradict her, and she did not seem to resent it.

In the meantime, Henri was eating his heart out with jealousy and sullen rage. The whole thing was unfair. He occasionally saw Paul, who boasted openly of his strong position in the Taillandier household, and he would not believe that Paul was not getting money out of the old lady as well as board and lodging. With no additional expenses Paul was better dressed than he used to be, and he looked fatter and better in health. All—or nearly all—of Henri's appeals, although pitched in a most pathetic key, were rebuffed. He felt a bitter hatred against his aunt, his brother, and life in general. If only she would die! What was the good of life to a woman at eighty-five or six? And, there was he—four young children, clamouring for food, and clothes, and the ordinary decent comforts. And, there was Paul, idling his days away at cafés and his nights at cabarets—nothing to do, and no responsibilities.

Meeting Paul one day he said:

'I say, old boy, couldn't you spring me a hundred francs? I haven't the money to pay my rent next week.'

'She gives me nothing,' replied Paul.

Henri did not believe this, but it would be undiplomatic to quarrel. He said:

'Aren't there—isn't there some little thing lying about the villa you could slip in your pocket? We could sell it, see? Go shares. I'm desperately pushed.'

Paul looked down his nose. Name of a pig! Did Henri think he had never thought of that? Many and many a time the temptation had come to him. But no; every few months people came from the lawyer's office, and the inventory of the whole household was checked. The servants could not be suspected. They were not selected without irreproachable characters. If he were suspected—well, all kinds of unpleasant things might crop up. Oh, no, he was too well off where he was. The game was to lie in wait. The old lady simply must die soon. She had even been complaining of her chest that morning. She was always playing with the perroquet. Somehow this bird got on Paul's nerves. He wanted to wring its neck. He imitated the way she would say: 'There's a pretty lady! Oh, my sweet! Another nice grape for my little one. There's a pretty lady!' He told Henri all about this, and the elder brother went on his way with a grunt that only conveyed doubt and suspicion.

In view of this position it seemed strange that in the end it was Paul who was directly responsible for the dénouement in the Taillandier household. His success went to his rather weak head like wine. He began to swagger and buster and abuse his aunt's hospitality. And, curiously enough, the more he advanced the further she withdrew. The eccentric old lady seemed to be losing her powers of resistance so far as he was concerned. And, he began to borrow small sums of money from her, and, as she acquiesced so readily, to increase his demands. He let his travelling business go, and sometimes he would get lost for days at a time. He would spend his time at the races, and drinking with doubtful acquaintances in obscure cafés. Sometimes he won, but in the majority of cases he lost. He ran up bills and got into debt. By cajoling small sums out of his aunt he kept his debtors at bay for nearly nine months.

But one evening he came to see Henri in a great state of distress. His face, which had taken on a healthier glow when he first went to live with his aunt, had become puffy and livid. His eyes were bloodshot.

'Old boy,' he said, 'I'm at my wits' end. I've got to find seven thousand francs by the twenty-first of the month, or they're going to foreclose. How do you stand? I'll pay you back.'

To try to borrow money from Henri was like appealing to the desert for a cooling draught. He also had to find money by the twenty-first, and he was overdrawn at the bank. They exchanged confidences, and in their mutual distress they felt sorry for each other and for themselves. It was a November evening, and the rain was driving along the boulevards in fitful gusts. After trudging a long way they turned into a little café in the Rue de la Roquette, and sat down and ordered two cognacs. The café was almost deserted. A few men in mackintoshes were scattered around reading the evening papers. They sat at a marble table in the corner and tried to think of ways and means. But after a time a silence fell between them. There seemed nothing more to suggest. They could hear the rain beating on the skylight. An old man four tables away was poring over *La Patrie*.

Suddenly, Henri looked furtively around the room and clutched his brother's arm.

'Paul!' he whispered.

'What is it?'

'Do you remember—it has all come back to me—suddenly—one night, a night something like this—it must be give or six years ago—we were seated here in this same café—do you remember?'

'No. I don't remember. What was it?'

'It was the night of that murder in the Landes district. We got talking about—don't you remember?'

Paul scratched his temple and sipped the cognac. Henri leant closer to him.

'You said—you said that if you lived with anyone, it was the easiest thing in the world to murder them. An accident, you know. And, you go screaming into the street—'

Paul started, and stared at his brother, who continued:

'You said that if ever you—you had to do it, you would guarantee that you would take every trouble. You wouldn't leave a trace behind.'

Paul was acting. He pretended to half-remember, to half-understand. But his eyes narrowed. Imbecile! Hadn't he been through it all in imagination a hundred times? Hadn't he already been planning and scheming an act for which his brother would reap half the benefit? Nevertheless, he was staggered. He never imagined that the suggestion would come from Henri. He was secretly relieved. If Henri was to receive half the benefit, let him also share half the responsibilities. The risk in any case would be wholly his. He grinned enigmatically, and they put their heads together. And so, in that dim corner of the café was planned the perfect murder.

Coining up against the actual proposition, Paul had long since realized that the affair was not so easy of accomplishment as he had so airily suggested. For the thing must be done without violence, without clues, without a trace. Such ideas as leaving the window open at night were out of the question, as the companion slept in the same room. Moreover, the old lady was quite capable of getting out of bed and shutting it herself if she felt a draught. Some kind of accident? Yes, but what? Suppose she slipped and broke her neck when Paul was in the room. It would be altogether too suspicious. Besides, she would probably only partially break her neck. She would regain sufficient consciousness to tell. To drown her in her bath? The door was always locked or the companion hovering around.

'You've always got to remember,' whispered Paul, 'if any suspicion falls on me, there's the motive. There's strong motive why I should—it's got to be absolutely untraceable. I don't care if some people do suspect afterwards—when we've got the money.'

'What about her food?'

'The food is cooked by Ernestine, and the companion serves it. Besides, suppose I got a chance to tamper with the food, how am I going to get hold of—you know?'

'Weed-killer?'

'Yes, I should he in a pretty position if they traced the fact that I had bought weed-killer. You might buy some and let me have a little on the quiet.

Henri turned pale. 'No, no; the motive applies to me, too. They'd get us both.'

When the two pleasant gentlemen parted at midnight their plans were still very immature, but they arranged to meet the following evening. It was the thirteenth of the month. To save the situation the deed must be accomplished within eight days. Of course, they wouldn't get the money at once, but, knowing the circumstances, creditors would be willing to wait. When they met the following evening in the Café des Sentiers, Paul appeared flushed and excited, and Henri was pale and on edge.

He hadn't slept. He wanted to wash the whole thing out.

'And, sell up your home, I suppose?' sneered Paul.

'Listen, my little cabbage. I've got it. Don't distress yourself. You proposed this last night. I've been thinking about it and watching for months. Ernestine is a good cook, and very methodical. Oh, very methodical! She does everything every day in the same way exactly to schedule. My apartment is on the same floor, so I am able to appreciate her punctuality and exactness. The old woman eats sparingly and according to routine. One night she has fish. The next night she has a soufflé made with two eggs. Fish, soufflé, fish, soufflé, regular as the beat of a clock. Now, listen. After lunch every day Ernestine washes up the plates and pans. After that she prepares roughly the evening meal. If it is a fish night, she prepares the fish ready to pop into the pan. If it is a soufflé night, she beats up two eggs and puts them ready in a basin. Having done that, she changes her frock, powders her nose, and goes over to the convent to see her sister who is working there. She is away an hour and a half. She returns punctually at four o'clock. You could set your watch by her movements.'

'Yes, but—'

'It is difficult to insert what I propose in fish, but I don't see any difficulty in dropping it into two beaten-up eggs, and giving an extra twist to the egg-whisk, or whatever they call it.'

Henri's face was quite grey.

'But—but—Paul, how are you going to get hold of the poison?'

'Who said anything about poison?'

'Well, but what?'

'That's where you come in.'

'Yes, you're in it, too, aren't you? You get half the spoils, don't you? Why shouldn't you—some time tomorrow when your wife's out—'

'What?'

'Just grind up a piece of glass.'

'Glass!'

'Yes, you've heard of glass, haven't you? An ordinary piece of broken wine-glass will do. Grind it up as fine as a powder, the finer the better, the finer the more-effective.'

Henri gasped. No, no, he couldn't do this thing. Very well, then; if he was such a coward Paul would have to do it himself. And perhaps, when the time came Henri would also be too frightened to draw his dividends. Perhaps, he would like to make them over to his dear brother Paul? Come, it was only a little thing to do. Eight days to the twenty-first. Tomorrow, fishday, but Wednesday would be soufflé. So easy, so untraceable, so safe.

'But you,' whined Henri, 'they will suspect you.'

'Even if they do they can prove nothing. But in order to avoid this unpleasantness I propose to leave home soon after breakfast. I shall return at a quarter-past three, letting myself in through the stable yard. The stables, as you know, are not used. There is no one else on that floor. Ernestine is upstairs. She only comes down to answer the front-door bell. I shall be in and out of the house within five minutes, and I shan't return till late at night, when perhaps—I may be too late to render assistance.'

Henri was terribly agitated. On one hand was—just murder, a thing he had never connected himself within his life. On the other hand was comfort for himself and his family, an experience he had given up hoping for. It was in any case not exactly murder on his part. It was Paul's murder. At the same time, knowing all about it, being an accessory before the fact, it would seem contemptible to a degree to put the whole onus on Paul. Grinding up a piece of glass was such a little thing. It couldn't possibly incriminate him. Nobody could ever prove that he'd done it. But it was a terrible step to take.

'Have another cognac, my little cabbage.'

It was Paul's voice that jerked him back to actuality. He said: 'All right, yes, yes,' but whether this referred to the cognac or to the act of grinding up a piece of glass he hardly knew himself.

From that moment to twenty-four hours later, when he handed over a white packet to his brother across the same table at the Café des Sentiers, Henri seemed to be in a nightmarish dream. He had no recollection of how he had passed the time. He seemed to pass from that last cognac to this one, and the interval was a blank.

'Fish today, soufflé tomorrow,' he heard Paul chuckling. 'Brother, you have done your work well.'

When Paul went he wanted to call after him to come back, but he was frightened of the sound of his own voice. He was terribly frightened. He went to bed very late and could not sleep. The next morning he awoke with a headache, and he got his wife to telegraph to the office to say that he was too ill to come. He lay in bed all day, visualizing over and over and over again the possible events of the evening.

Paul would be caught. Someone would catch him actually putting the powder into the eggs. He would be arrested. Paul would give him away. Why did Paul say it was so easy to murder anyone if you lived with them? It wasn't easy at all. The whole thing was chock-a-block with dangers and pitfalls. Pitfalls! At half-past three he started up in bed. He had a vision of himself and Paul being guillotined side by side! He must stop it at any cost. He began to get up. Then he realized that it was already too late. The deed had been done. Paul had said that he would be in and out of the house within five minutes at three-fifteen—a quarter of an hour ago! Where was Paul? Would he be coming to see him? He was going to spend the evening out somewhere, 'returning late at night'.

He dressed feverishly. There was still time. He could call at his aunt's. Rush down to the kitchen, seize the basin of beaten-up eggs, and throw them away. But where? How? By the time he got there Ernestine would have returned. She would want to know all about it. The egg mixture would be examined, analysed. God in Heaven! It was too late! The thing would have to go on, and he suffer and wait.

Having dressed, he went out after saying to his wife: 'It's all right. It's going to be all right,' not exactly knowing what he meant. He walked rapidly along the streets with no fixed destination in his mind. He found himself in the Café Rue de la Roquette, where the idea was first conceived, where he had reminded his brother.

He sat there drinking, waiting for the hours to pass.

Soufflé day, and the old lady dined at seven! It was now not quite five. He hoped Paul would turn up. A stranger tried to engage him in conversation. The stranger apparently had some grievance against a railway company. He wanted to tell him all the details about a contract for rivets, over which he had been disappointed. Henri didn't understand a word he was talking about. He didn't listen. He wanted the stranger to drop down dead or vanish into thin air. At last he called the waiter and paid for his reckoning, indicated by a small pile of saucers. From there he walked rapidly to the Café des Sentiers, looking for Paul. He was not there. Six o'clock. One hour more. He could not keep still. He paid and went on again, calling at café after café. A quarter to seven. Pray God that she threw it away. Had he ground it fine enough?

Five minutes to seven. Seven o'clock. Now. He picked up his hat and went again. The brandy had gone to his head. At half-past seven he laughed recklessly. After all, what was the good of life to this old woman of eighty-six? He tried to convince himself that he had done it for the sake of his wife and children. He tried to concentrate on the future, how he could manage on eight or ten thousand francs a year. He would give notice at the office, be rude to people who had been bullying him for years—that old blackguard Mocquin!

At ten o'clock he was drunk, torpid, and indifferent. The whole thing was over for good or ill. What did it matter? He terribly wanted to see Paul, but he was too tired to care very much. The irrevocable step had been taken. He went home to bed and fell into a heavy drunken sleep.

'Henri! Henri, wake up! What is the matter with you?' His wife was shaking him. He blinked his way into a partial condition of consciousness. November sunlight was pouring into the room.

'It's late, isn't it?' he said, involuntarily.

'It's past eight. You'll be late at the office. You didn't go yesterday. If you go on like this you'll get the sack, and then what shall we do?'

Slowly the recollection of last night's events came back to him.

'There's nothing to worry about,' he said. 'I'm too ill to go today. Send them another telegram. It'll be all right.'

His wife looked at him searchingly. 'You've been drinking,' she said. 'Oh, you men! God knows what will become of us.'

She appeared to be weeping in her apron. It struck him forcibly at that instant how provoking and small women are. Here was Jeannette crying over her petty troubles. Whereas he—

The whole thing was becoming vivid again. Where was Paul? What had happened? Was it at all likely that he could go down to an office on a day like this, a day that was to decide his fate?

He groaned, and elaborated rather pathetically his imaginary ailments, anything to keep this woman quiet. She left him at last, and he lay there waiting for something to happen. The hours passed. What would be the first intimation? Paul or the gendarmes? Thoughts of the latter stirred him to a state of fevered activity. About midday he arose, dressed, and went out. He told his wife he was going to the office, but he had no intention of doing so. He went and drank coffee at a place up in the Marais. He was terrified of his old haunts. He wandered from place to place, uncertain how to act. Late in the afternoon he entered a café in the Rue Alibert. At a kiosk outside he bought a late edition of an afternoon newspaper. He sat down, ordered a drink and opened the newspaper. He glanced at the central news page, and as his eye absorbed one paragraph he unconsciously uttered a low scream. The paragraph was as follows:

> Mysterious Affair at Chantilly
>
> A mysterious affair occurred at Chantilly this morning. A middle-aged man, named Paul Denoyel, complained of pains in the stomach after eating an omelette. He died soon after in great agony. He was staying with his aunt, Mme Taillandier. No other members of the household were affected. The matter is to be inquired into.

The rest was a dream. He was only vaguely conscious of the events which followed. He wandered through it all, the instinct of self-preservation bidding him hold his tongue in all circumstances. He knew nothing. He had seen nothing. He had a visionary recollection of a plump, weeping Ernestine, at the inquest, enlarging upon the eccentricities of her mistress. A queer woman, who would brook no contradiction. He heard a lot about the fish day and the soufflé day, and how the old lady insisted that this was a fish day, and, and that she had had a soufflé the day before. You could not argue with her when she was like that. And, Ernestine had beaten up the eggs all ready for the soufflé-most provoking! But Ernestine was a good cook, of method and economy. She wasted nothing. What should she do with the eggs? Why, of course, Mr Paul, who since he had come to live there was never content with a *café cornplet*. He must have a breakfast, like these English and other foreigners do. She made him an omelette, which he ate heartily.

Then the beaten-up eggs with their deadly mixture were intended for Mme Taillandier? But who was responsible for this? Ernestine? But there was no motive here. Ernestine gained nothing by her mistress's death. Indeed she only stood to lose her situation. The inquiry went on a long while. Henri himself was conscious of being in the witness-box. He knew nothing. He couldn't understand it. His brother would not be likely to do that. He himself was prostrate with grief. He loved his brother.

There was nothing to do but return an open verdict. Shadowy figures passed before his mind's eye—shadowy figures and shadowy realizations. He had perfectly murdered his brother. The whole of the dividends of the estate would one day be his, and his wife's and children's. Eighteen thousand francs a year! One day—

One vision more vivid than the rest—the old lady on the day following the inquest, seated bolt upright at her table, like a figure of perpetuity, playing with the old grey perroquet, stroking its mangy neck.

'There's a pretty lady! Oh, my sweet! Another nice grape for my little one. There's a pretty lady!'

A FACE IN THE DARK

Ruskin Bond

It may give you some idea of rural humour if I begin this tale with an anecdote that concerns me. I was walking alone through a village at night when I met an old man carrying a lantern. I found, to my surprise, that the man was blind. 'Old man,' I asked, 'if you cannot see, why do you carry a lamp?'

'I carry this,' he replied, 'so that fools do not stumble against me in the dark.'

This incident has only a slight connection with the story that follows, but I think it provides the right sort of tone and setting. Mr Oliver, an Anglo-Indian teacher, was returning to his school late one night, on the outskirts of the hill-station of Simla. The school was conducted on English public school lines and the boys, most of them from well-to-do Indian families, wore blazers, caps and ties. *Life* magazine, in a feature on India had once called this school the 'Eton of the East'.

Individuality was not encouraged; they were all destined to become 'leaders of men'.

Mr Oliver had been teaching in the school for several years. Sometimes it seemed like an eternity; for one day followed another with the same monotonous routine. The Simla bazaar, with its cinemas and restaurants, was about two miles from the school; and Mr Oliver, a bachelor, usually strolled into the town in the evening, returning after dark, when he would take a short cut through a pine forest.

When there was a strong wind, the pine trees made sad, eerie sounds that kept most people to the main road. But Mr Oliver was not a nervous or imaginative man. He carried a torch and, on the night I write of, its pale gleam—the batteries were running down—moved fitfully over the narrow forest path. When its flickering light fell on the figure of a boy, who was sitting alone on a rock, Mr Oliver stopped. Boys were not supposed to be out of school after 7 p.m., and it was now well past nine.

'What are you doing out here, boy?' asked Mr Oliver sharply, moving closer so that he could recognize the miscreant. But even as he approached the boy, Mr Oliver sensed that something was wrong. The boy appeared to be crying. His head hung down, he held his face in his hands, and his body shook convulsively. It was a strange, soundless weeping, and Mr Oliver felt distinctly uneasy.

'Well—what's the matter?' he asked, his anger giving way to concern. 'What are you crying for?' The boy would not answer or look up. His body continued to be racked with silent sobbing.

'Come on, boy, you shouldn't be out here at this hour. Tell me the trouble. Look up!'

The boy looked up. He took his hands from his face and looked up at his teacher. The light from Mr Oliver's torch fell on the boy's face—if you could call it a face.

He had no eyes, ears, nose, or mouth. It was just a round, smooth head—with a school cap on top of it. And that's where the story should end—as indeed it has for several people who have had similar experiences and dropped dead of inexplicable heart attacks. But for Mr Oliver it did not end there.

The torch fell from his trembling hand. He turned and scrambled down the path, running blindly through the trees and calling for help. He was still running towards the school building when he saw a lantern swinging in the middle of the path. Mr Oliver had never before been so pleased to see the night-watchman. He stumbled up to the watchman, gasping for breath and speaking incoherently.

'What is it, Sir?' asked the watchman. 'Has there been an accident? Why are you running?'

'I saw something—something horrible—a boy weeping in the forest—and he had no face!'

'No face, Sir?'

'No eyes, nose, mouth—nothing.'

'Do you mean it was like this, Sir?' asked the watchman, and raised the lamp to his own face. The watchman had no eyes, no ears, no features at all—not even an eyebrow!

The wind blew the lamp out, and Mr Oliver had his heart attack.

THE VOICE IN THE NIGHT

W.H. Hodgson

It was a dark, starless night. We were becalmed in the Northern Pacific. Our exact position I do not know; for the sun had been hidden during the course of a weary, breathless week, by a thin haze which had seemed to float above us, about the height of our mastheads, at whiles descending and shrouding the surrounding sea.

With there being no wind, we had steadied the tiller, and I was the only man on deck. The crew, consisting of two men and a boy, were sleeping forrard in their den; while Will—my friend, and the master of our little craft-was aft in his bunk on the port side of the little cabin.

Suddenly, from out of the surrounding darkness, there came a hail:

'Schooner, ahoy!'

The cry was so unexpected that I gave no immediate answer, because of my surprise.

It came again—a voice curiously throaty and inhuman, calling from somewhere upon the dark sea away on our port broadside:

'Schooner, ahoy!'

'Hullo!' I sung out, having gathered my wits somewhat. 'What are you? What do you want?'

'You need not be afraid,' answered the queer voice, having probably noticed some trace of confusion in my tone. 'I am only an old—man.'

The pause sounded oddly; but it was only afterwards that it came back to me with any significance.

'Why don't you come alongside, then?' I queried somewhat snappishly; for I liked not his hinting at my having been a trifle shaken.

'I—I—can't. It wouldn't be safe. I—' The voice broke off, and there was silence.

'What do you mean?' I asked, growing more and more astonished. 'Why not safe? Where are you?'

I listened for a moment; but there came no answer. And then, a sudden indefinite suspicion, of I knew not what, coming to me, I stepped swiftly to the binnacle, and took out the lighted lamp. At the same time, I knocked on the deck with my heel to waken Will. Then I was back at the side, throwing the yellow funnel of light out into the silent immensity beyond our rail. As I did so, I heard a slight, muffled cry, and then the sound of a splash as though some one had dipped oars abruptly. Yet I cannot say that I saw anything with certainty; save, it seemed to me, that with the first flash of the light, there had been something upon the waters, where now there was nothing.

'Hullo, there!' I called. 'What foolery is this!'

But there came only the indistinct sounds of a boat being pulled away into the night.

Then I heard Will's voice, from the direction of the after scuttle:

'What's up, George?'

'Come here, Will!' I said.

'What is it?' he asked, coming across the deck.

I told him the queer thing which had happened. He put several questions; then after a moment's silence, he raised his hands to his lips, and hailed:

'Boat, ahoy!'

From a long distance away there came back to us a faint reply, and my companion repeated his call. Presently, after a short period of silence, there grew on our hearing the muffled sound of oars; at which Will hailed again.

This time there was a reply:

'Put away the light.'

'I'm damned if I will,' I muttered; but Will told me to do as the voice bade, and I shoved it down under the bulwarks.

'Come nearer,' he said, and the oar-strokes continued. Then, when apparently some half-dozen fathoms distant, they again ceased.

'Come alongside,' exclaimed Will. 'There's nothing to be frightened of aboard here!'

'Promise that you will not show the light?'

'What's to do with you,' I burst out, 'that you're so infernally afraid of the light?'

'Because—' began the voice, and stopped short.

'Because what?' I asked quickly.

Will put his hand on my shoulder.

'Shut up a minute, old man,' he said, in a low voice. 'Let me tackle him.'

He leant more over the rail.

'See here, Mister,' he said, 'this is a pretty queer business, you coming upon us like this, right out in the middle of the blessed Pacific. How are we to know what sort of a hanky-panky trick you're up to? You say there's only one of you. How are we to know, unless we get a squint at you—eh? What's your objection to the light, anyway?'

As he finished, I heard the noise of the oars again, and then the voice came; but now from a greater distance, and sounding extremely hopeless and pathetic.

'I am sorry—sorry! I would not have troubled you, only I am hungry, and—so is she.'

The voice died away, and the sound of the oars, dipping irregularly, was borne to us.

'Stop!' sung out Will. 'I don't want to drive you away. Come back! We'll keep the light hidden, if you don't like it.'

He turned to me:

'It's a damned queer rig, this; but I think there's nothing to be afraid of?'

There was a question in his tone, and I replied:

'No, I think the poor devil's been wrecked around here, and gone crazy.'

The sound of the oars drew nearer.

'Shove that lamp back in the binnacle,' said Will; then he leaned over the rail and listened. I replaced the lamp, and came back to his side. The dipping of the oars ceased some dozen yards distant.

'Won't you come alongside now?' asked Will in an even voice. 'I have had the lamp put back in the binnacle.'

'I—I cannot,' replied the voice. 'I dare not come nearer. I dare not even pay you for the—the provisions.'

'That's all right,' said Will, and hesitated. 'You're welcome to as much grub as you can take—' Again he hesitated.

'You are very good,' exclaimed the voice. 'May God, Who understands everything, reward you—' It broke off huskily.

'The—the lady?' said Will abruptly. 'Is she—'

'I have left her behind upon the island,' came the voice.

'What island?' I cut in.

'I know not its name,' returned the voice. 'I would to God—!' it began, and checked itself as suddenly.

'Could we not send a boat for her?' asked Will at this point.

'No!' said the voice, with extraordinary emphasis. 'My God!

No!' There was a moment's pause; then it added, in a tone which seemed a merited reproach:

'It was because of our want I ventured—because her agony tortured me.'

'I am a forgetful brute,' exclaimed Will. 'Just wait a minute, whoever you are, and I will bring you up something at once.'

In a couple of minutes he was back again, and his arms were full of various edibles. He paused at the rail.

'Can't you come alongside for them?' he asked.

'No—I *dare not,*' replied the voice, and it seemed to me that in its tones I detected a note of stifled craving—as though the owner hushed a mortal desire. It came to me then in a flash, that the poor old creature out there in the darkness, was *suffering* for actual need of that which Will held in his arms; and yet, because of some unintelligible dread, refraining from dashing to the side of our little schooner, and receiving it. And with the lightning-like conviction, there came the knowledge that the Invisible was not mad; but sanely facing some intolerable horror.

'Damn it, Will!' I said, full of many feelings, over which predominated a vast sympathy. 'Get a box. We must float off the stuff to him in it.'

This we did—propelling it away from the vessel, out into the darkness, by means of a boathook. In a minute, a slight cry from the Invisible came to us, and we knew that he had secured the box.

A little later, he called out a farewell to us, and so heartful a blessing, that I am sure we were the better for it. Then, without more ado, we heard the ply of oars across the darkness.

'Pretty soon off,' remarked Will, with perhaps just a little sense of injury.

'Wait,' I replied. 'I think somehow he'll come back. He must have been badly needing that food.'

'And the lady,' said Will. For a moment he was silent; then he continued:

'It's the queerest thing ever I've tumbled across, since I've been fishing.'

'Yes,' I said, and fell to pondering.

And so the time slipped away—an hour, another, and still Will stayed with me; for the queer adventure had knocked all desire for sleep out of him.

The third hour was three parts through, when we heard again the sound of oars across the silent ocean.

'Listen!' said Will, a low note of excitement in his voice.

'He's coming, just as I thought,' I muttered.

The dipping of the oars grew nearer, and I noted that the strokes were firmer and longer. The food had been needed.

They came to a stop a little distance off the broadside, and the queer voice came again to us through the darkness:

'Schooner, ahoy!'

'That you?' asked Will.

'Yes,' replied the voice. 'I left you suddenly; but—but there was great need.'

'The lady?' questioned Will.

'The—lady is grateful now on earth. She will be more grateful soon in—in heaven.'

Will began to make some reply, in a puzzled voice; but became confused, and broke off short. I said nothing. I was wondering at the curious pauses, and, apart from my wonder, I was full of a great sympathy.

The voice continued:

'We—she and I, have talked, as we shared the result of God's tenderness and yours—'

Will interposed; but without coherence.

'I beg of you not to—to belittle your deed of Christian

charity this night,' said the voice. 'Be sure that it has not escaped His notice.'

It stopped, and there was a full minute's silence. Then it came again:

'We have spoken together upon that which—which has befallen us. We had thought to go out, without telling any, of the terror which has come into our lives. She is with me in believing that tonight's happenings are under a special ruling, and that it is God's wish that we should tell to you all that we have suffered since—since—'

'Yes?' said Will softly.

'Since the sinking of the *Albatross.*'

'Ah!' I exclaimed involuntarily. 'She left Newcastle for 'Frisco some six months ago, and hasn't been heard of since.'

'Yes,' answered the voice. 'But some few degrees to the North of the line she was caught in a terrible storm, and dismasted. When the day came, it was found that she was leaking badly, and, presently, it falling to a calm, the sailors took to the boats, leaving—leaving a young lady—my fiancèe—and myself upon the wreck.

'We were below, gathering together a few of our belongings, when they left. They were entirely callous, through fear, and when we came up upon the decks, we saw them only as small shapes afar off upon the horizon. Yet we did not despair, but set to work and constructed a small raft. Upon this we put such few matters as it would hold, including a quantity of water and some ship's biscuit. Then, the vessel being very deep in the water, we got ourselves on to the raft, and pushed off.

'It was later, when I observed that we seemed to be in the way of some tide or current which bore us from the ship at an angle; so that in the course of three hours, by my watch, her hull became invisible to our sight, her broken masts remaining in view for a somewhat longer period. Then, toward evening, it grew misty, and so through the night. The next day we were still encompassed by the mist, the weather remaining quiet.

'For four days we drifted through this strange haze, until, on the evening of the fourth day, there grew upon our ears the murmur of breakers at a distance. Gradually it became plainer, and, somewhat after midnight, it appeared to sound upon either hand at no very great space. The raft was raised upon a swell several times, and then we were in smooth water, and the noise of the breakers was behind.

'When the morning came, we found that we were in a sort of great lagoon; but of this we noticed little at the time; for close before us, through the enshrouding mist, loomed the hull of a large sailing-vessel. With one accord, we fell upon our knees and thanked God; for we thought that here was an end to our perils. We had much to learn.

'The raft drew near to the ship, and we shouted on them to take us aboard; but none answered. Presently the raft touched against the side of the vessel, and, seeing a rope hanging downwards, I seized it and began to climb. Yet I had much ado to make my way up, because of a kind of grey, lichenous fungus which had seized upon the rope, and which blotched the side of the ship lividly.

'I reached the rail and clambered over it, on to the deck. Here I saw that the decks were covered, in great patches, with the grey masses, some of them rising into nodules several feet in height; but at the time I thought less of this matter than of the possibility of there being people aboard the ship. I shouted; but none answered. Then I went to the door below the poop deck. I opened it, and peered in. There was a great smell of staleness, so that I knew in a moment that nothing living was within, and with the knowledge, I shut the door quickly; for I felt suddenly lonely.

'I went back to the side where I had scrambled up. My—my sweetheart was still sitting quietly upon the raft. Seeing me look down, she called up to know whether there were any aboard of the ship. I replied that the vessel had the appearance of having been long deserted; but that if she would wait a little I would see whether there was anything in the shape of a ladder by which she could ascend to the deck. Then we would make a search through the vessel together. A little later on the opposite side of the decks, I found a rope side-ladder. This I carried across, and a minute afterwards she was beside me.

'Together we explored the cabins and apartments in the after part of the ship; but nowhere was there any sign of life. Here and there, within the cabins themselves, we came across odd patches of that queer fungus; but this, as my sweetheart said, could be cleansed away.

'In the end, having assured ourselves that the after portion of the vessel was empty, we picked our ways to the bows, between the ugly grey nodules of that strange growth; and here we made a further search, which told us that there was indeed none aboard but ourselves.

'This being now beyond any doubt, we returned to the stern of the ship and proceeded to make ourselves as comfortable as possible. Together we cleared out and cleaned two of the cabins; and after that I made examination whether there was anything eatable in the ship. This I soon found was so, and thanked God in my heart for His goodness. In addition to this I discovered the whereabouts of the freshwater pump, and having fixed it I found the water drinkable, though somewhat unpleasant to the taste.

'For several days we stayed aboard the ship, without attempting to get to the shore. We were busily engaged in making the place habitable. Yet even thus early we became aware that our lot was even less to be desired than might have been imagined; for though, as a first step, we scraped away the odd patches of growth that studded the floors and walls of the cabins and saloon, yet they returned almost to their original size within the space of twenty-four hours, which not only discouraged us, but gave us a feeling of vague unease.

'Still we would not admit ourselves beaten, so set to work afresh, and not only scraped away the fungus, but soaked the places where it had been, with carbolic, a can-full of which I had found in the pantry. Yet, by the end of the week the growth had returned in full strength, and, in addition, it had spread to other places, as though our touching it had allowed germs from it to travel elsewhere.

'On the seventh morning, my sweetheart woke to find a small patch of it growing on her pillow, close to her face. At that, she came to me, so soon as she could get her garments upon her. I was in the galley at the time lighting the fire for breakfast.

'"Come here, John," she said, and led me aft. When I saw the thing upon her pillow I shuddered, and then and there we agreed to go right out of the ship and see whether we could not fare to make ourselves more comfortable ashore.

'Hurriedly we gathered together our few belongings, and even among these I found that the fungus had been at work; for one of her shawls had a little lump of it growing near one edge. I threw the whole thing over the side, without saying anything to her.

'The raft was still alongside, but it was too clumsy to guide, and I lowered down a small boat that hung across the stern, and in this we made our way to the shore. Yet, as we drew near to it, I became gradually aware that here the vile fungus, which had driven us from the ship, was growing riot. In places it rose into horrible, fantastic mounds, which seemed almost to quiver, as with a quiet life, when the wind blew across them. Here and there it took on the forms of vast fingers, and in others it just spread out flat and smooth and treacherous. Odd places, it appeared as grotesque stunted trees, seeming extraordinarily kinked and gnarled—the whole quaking vilely at times.

'At first, it seemed to us that there was no single portion of the surrounding shore which was not hidden beneath the masses of the hideous lichen; yet, in this, I found we were mistaken; for somewhat later, coasting along the shore at a little distance, we descried a smooth white patch of what appeared to be fine sand, and there we landed. It was not sand. What it was I do not know. All that I have observed is that upon it the fungus will not grow; while everywhere else, save where the sand-like earth wanders oddly, path-wise, amid the grey desolation of the lichen, there is nothing but that loathsome greyness.

'It is difficult to make you understand how cheered we were to find one place that was absolutely free from the growth, and here we deposited our belongings. Then we went back to the ship for such things as it seemed to us we should need. Among other matters, I managed to bring ashore with me one of the ship's sails, with which I constructed two small tents, which, though exceedingly rough-shaped, served the purposes for which they were intended. In these we lived and stored our various necessities, and thus for a matter of some four weeks all went smoothly and without particular unhappiness. Indeed, I may say with much of happiness—for—for we were together.

'It was on the thumb of her right hand that the growth first showed. It was only a small circular spot, much like a little grey mole. My God! how the fear leapt to my heart when she showed me the place. We cleansed it, between us, washing it with carbolic and water. In the morning of the following day she showed her hand to me again. The grey warty thing had returned. For a little while, we looked at one another in silence. Then, still wordless, we started again to remove it. In the midst of the operation she spoke suddenly.

'"What's that on the side of your face, dear?" Her voice was sharp with anxiety. I put my hand up to feel.

'"There! Under the hair by your ear. A little to the front a bit." My finger rested upon the place, and then I knew.

'"Let us get your thumb done first," I said. And she submitted, only because she was afraid to touch me until it was cleansed. I finished washing and disinfecting her thumb, and then she turned to my face. After it was finished we sat together and talked awhile of many things; for there had come into our lives sudden, very terrible thoughts. We were, all at once, afraid of something worse than death. We spoke of loading the boat with provisions and water and making our way out on to the sea; yet we were helpless, for many causes, and—and the growth had attacked us already. We decided to stay. God would do with us what was His will. We would wait.

'A month, two months, three months passed and the places grew somewhat, and there had come others. Yet we fought so strenuously with the fear that its headway was but slow, comparatively speaking.

'Occasionally we ventured off to the ship for such stores as we needed. There we found that the fungus grew persistently. One of the nodules on the maindeck became soon as high as my head.

'We had now given up all thought or hope of leaving the island. We had realised that it would be unallowable to go among healthy humans, with the things from which we were suffering.

'With this determination and knowledge in our minds we knew that we should have to husband our food and water; for we did not know, at that time, but that we should possibly live for many years.

'This reminds me that I have told you that I am an old man. Judged by years this is not so. But-but-'

He broke off; then continued somewhat abruptly:

'As I was saying, we knew that we should have to use care in the matter of food. But we had no idea then how little food there was left, of which to take care. It was a week later that I made the discovery that all the other bread tanks—which I had supposed full—were empty, and that (beyond odd tins of vegetables and meat, and some other matters) we had nothing on which to depend, but the bread in the tank which I had already opened.

'After learning this I bestirred myself to do what I could, and set to work at fishing in the lagoon; but with no success. At this I was somewhat inclined to feel desperate until the thought came to me to try outside the lagoon, in the open sea.

'Here, at times, I caught odd fish; but so infrequently that they proved of but little help in keeping us from the hunger which threatened. It seemed to me that our deaths were likely to come by hunger, and not by the growth of the thing which had seized upon our bodies.

'We were in this state of mind when the fourth month wore out. Then I made a very horrible discovery. One morning, a little before midday, I came off from the ship with a portion of the biscuits which were left. In the mouth of her tent I saw my sweetheart sitting, eating something.

'"What is it, my dear?" I called out as I leapt ashore. Yet, on hearing my voice, she seemed confused, and, turning, slyly threw something towards the edge of the little clearing. It fell short, and a vague suspicion having arisen within me, I walked across and picked it up. It was a piece of the grey fungus.

'As I went to her with it in my hand, she turned deadly pale; then a rose red.

'I felt strangely dazed and frightened.

'"My dear! My dear!" I said, and could say no more. Yet at my words she broke down and cried bitterly. Gradually, as she calmed, I got from her the news that she had tried it the preceding day, and—and liked it. I got her to promise on her knees not to touch it again, however great our hunger. After she had promised she told me that the desire for it had come suddenly, and that, until the moment of desire, she had experienced nothing towards it but the most extreme repulsion.

'Later in the day, feeling strangely restless, and much shaken with the thing which I had discovered, I made my way along one of the twisted paths—formed by the white, sand-like substance—which led among the fungoid growth. I had, once before, ventured along there; but not to any great distance. This time, being involved in perplexing thought, I went much farther than hitherto.

'Suddenly I was called to myself by a queer, hoarse sound on my left. Turning quickly I saw that there was movement among an extraordinarily shaped mass of fungus, close to my elbow. It was swaying uneasily, as though it possessed life of its own. Abruptly, as I stared, the thought came to me that the thing had a grotesque resemblance to the figure of a distorted human creature. Even as the fancy flashed into my brain, there was a slight, sickening noise of tearing, and I saw that one of the branch-like arms was detaching itself from the surrounding grey masses, and coming towards me. The head of the thing—a shapeless grey ball, inclined in my direction. I stood stupidly, and the vile arm brushed across my face. I gave out a frightened cry, and ran back a few paces. There was a sweetish taste upon my lips where the thing had touched me. I licked them, and was immediately filled with an inhuman desire. I turned and seized a mass of the fungus. Then more, and—more. I was insatiable. In the midst of devouring, the remembrance of the morning's discovery swept into my mazed brain. It was sent by God. I dashed the fragment I held to the ground. Then, utterly wretched and feeling a dreadful guiltiness, I made my way back to the little encampment.

'I think she knew, by some marvellous intuition which love must have given, so soon as she set eyes on me. Her quiet sympathy made it easier for me, and I told her of my sudden weakness; yet omitted to mention the extraordinary thing which had gone before. I desired to spare her all unnecessary terror.

'But, for myself, I had added an intolerable knowledge, to breed an incessant terror in my brain; for I doubted not but that I had seen the end of one of those men who had come to the island in the ship in the lagoon; and in that monstrous ending I had seen our own.

'Thereafter we kept from the abominable food, though the desire for it had entered into our blood. Yet our drear punishment was upon us; for, day by day, with monstrous rapidity, the fungoid growth took hold of our poor bodies. Nothing we could do would check it materially, and so—and so—we who had been human, became—well, it matters less each day. Only—only we had been man and maid!

And day by day, the fight is more dreadful, to withstand the hunger-lust for the terrible lichen.

'A week ago we ate the last of the biscuit, and since that time I have caught three fish. I was out here fishing tonight, when your schooner drifted upon me out of the mist. I hailed you. You know the rest, and may God, out of His great heart, bless you for your goodness to a—a couple of poor outcast souls.'

There was the dip of an oar—another. Then the voice

came again, and for the last time, sounding through the slight surrounding mist, ghostly and mournful.

'God bless you! Goodbye.'

'Goodbye,' we shouted together, hoarsely, our hearts full of many emotions. I glanced about me. I became aware that the dawn was upon us.

The sun flung a stray beam across the hidden sea; pierced the mist dully, and lit up the receding boat with a gloomy fire. Indistinctly, I saw something nodding between the oars. I thought of a sponge—a great, grey nodding sponge. The oars continued to ply. They were grey—as was the boat—and my eyes searched a moment vainly for the conjunction of hand and oar. My gaze flashed back to the—head. It nodded forward as the oars went backward for the stroke. Then the oars were dipped, the boat shot out of the patch of light, and the—the thing went nodding into the mist.

CAULFIELD'S CRIME

Alice Perrin

Caulfield was a sulky, bad-tempered individual who made no friends and was deservedly unpopular, but he had the reputation of being the finest shot in the Punjab, and of possessing a knowledge of sporting matters that was almost superhuman. He was an extremely jealous shot, and hardly ever invited a companion to join him on his shooting trips, so it may be understood that I was keenly alive to the honour conferred on me when he suddenly asked me to go out for three days' small game shooting with him.

'I know a string of jheels,' he said, 'about thirty miles from here, where the duck and snipe must swarm. I marked the place down when I was out last month, and I've made arrangements to go there next Friday morning. You can come, too, if you like.'

I readily accepted the ungracious invitation, though I could hardly account for it, knowing his solitary ways, except that he probably thought that I was unlikely to assert myself, being but a youngster, and also he knew me better than he did most people, for our houses were next door, and I often strolled over to examine his enormous collection of skins and horns and other sporting trophies.

I bragged about the coming expedition in the club that evening, and was well-snubbed by two or three men who would have given anything to know the whereabouts of Caulfield's string of jheels, and who spitefully warned me to be careful that Caulfield did not end by shooting me.

'I believe he'd kill any chap who annoyed him,' said one of them, looking round to make sure that Caulfield was not at hand. 'I never met such a nasty-tempered fellow, I believe he's mad. But he can shoot, and what he doesn't know about game isn't worth knowing.'

Caulfield and I rode out the thirty miles early on the Friday morning, having sent our camp on ahead the previous night. We found our tents pitched in the scanty shade of some stunted dak jungle trees with thick dry bark, flat, shapeless leaves, that clattered together when stirred by the wind, and wicked-looking red blossoms. It was not a cheerful spot, and the soil was largely mixed with salt which had worked its way in white patches to the surface, and only encouraged the growth of the rankest of grass.

Before us stretched a dreary outlook of shallow lake and swampy ground, broken by dark patches of reeds and little bushy islands, while on the left a miserable mud village overlooked the water. The sun had barely cleared away the thick, heavy mist, which was still slowly rising here and there, and the jheel birds were wading majestically in search of their breakfast of small fish, and uttering harsh, discordant cries.

To my astonishment, Caulfield seemed a changed man. He was in excellent spirits, his eyes were bright, and the sullen frown had gone from his forehead.

'Isn't it a lovely spot?' he said, laughing and rubbing his hands. 'Beyond that village the snipe ought to rise in thousands from the rice fields. We shan't be able to shoot it all in three days, worse luck, but we'll keep it dark, and come again. Let's have breakfast. I don't want to lose any time.'

Half an hour later we started, our guns over our shoulders, and a couple of servants behind us carrying the luncheon and cartridge bags. My spirits rose with Caulfield's, for I felt we had the certainty of an excellent day's sport before us.

But the birds were unaccountably wild and few and far between, and luck seemed dead against us. 'Some brutes' had evidently been there before us and harried the birds, was Caulfield's opinion, delivered with disappointed rage, and after tramping and wading all day, we returned, weary and crestfallen, with only a few couple of snipe and half a dozen teal between us. Caulfield was so angry he could hardly eat any dinner, and afterwards sat cursing his luck and the culprits who had forestalled us, till we could neither of us keep awake any longer.

The next morning we took a different route from the previous day, but with no better result. On and on, and round and round we tramped, with only an occasional shot here and there, and at last, long after midday, we sat wearily down to eat our luncheon. I was ravenously hungry, and greedily devoured my share of the provisions, but Caulfield hardly touched a mouthful, and only sat moodily examining his gun, and taking long pulls from his whisky flask. We were seated on the roots of a large tamarind tree, close to the village, and the place had a dreary, depressing appearance. The yellow mud walls were ruined and crumbling, and the inhabitants seemed scanty and poverty-stricken. Two ragged old women were squatting a short distance off, watching us with dim, apathetic eyes, and a few naked children were playing near them, while some bigger boys were driving two or three lean buffaloes towards the water.

Presently another figure came in sight—a fakir, or mendicant priest, as was evident by the tawny masses of wool woven amongst his own black locks and hanging in ropes below his shoulders, the ashes smeared over the almost naked body, and the hollow gourd for alms which he held in his hand. The man's face was long and thin, and his pointed teeth glistened in the sunlight as he demanded money in a dismal monotone. Caulfield flung a pebble at him and told him roughly to be off, with the result that the man slowly disappeared behind a clump of tall, feathery grass.

'Did you notice that brute's face?' said Caulfield as we rose to start again. 'He must have been a pariah dog in a former existence. He was exactly like one!'

'Or a jackal perhaps,' I answered carelessly. 'He looked more like a wild beast.'

Then we walked on, skirting the village and plunging into the damp, soft rice fields. We put up a wisp of snipe, which we followed till we had shot them nearly all, and then, to our joy, we heard a rush of wings overhead, and a lot of duck went down into the corner of a jheel in front of us.

'We've got 'em!' said Caulfield, and we hurried on till we were almost within shot of the birds, and could hear them calling to each other in their fancied security. But suddenly they rose again in wild confusion, and with loud cries of alarm were out of range in a second. Caulfield swore, and so did I, and our rage was increased tenfold when the disturber of the birds appeared in sight, and proved to be the fakir who had paid us a visit at luncheon-time. Caulfield shook his fist at the man and abused him freely in Hindustani but without moving a muscle of his dog-like face the fakir passed us and continued on his way.

Words could not describe Caulfield's vexation.

'They were pin-tail, all of them,' he said, 'and the first decent chance we've had since we came out. To think of that beastly fakir spoiling the whole show, and I don't suppose he had the least idea what he had done.'

'Probably not,' I replied, 'unless there was some spite in it because you threw a stone at him that time.'

'Well, come along,' said Caulfield, with resignation, 'we

must make haste as it will be dark soon, and I want to try a place over by those palms before we knock off. We may as well let the servants go back as they've had a hard day. Have you got some cartridges in your pocket?'

'Yes, plenty,' I answered, and after despatching the two men back to the camp with what little game we had got, we walked on in silence.

The sun was sinking in a red ball and the air was heavy with damp, as the white mist stole slowly over the still, cold jheels. Far overhead came the first faint cackle of the wild geese returning home for the night, and presently as we approached the clump of palms we saw more water glistening between the rough stems, and on it, to our delight, a multitude of duck and teal.

But the next moment there was a whir-r-r of wings like the rumble of thunder, and a dense mass of birds flew straight into the air and wheeled bodily away, while the sharp, cold atmosphere resounded with their startled cries. Caulfield said nothing, but he set his jaw and walked rapidly forward, while I followed. We skirted the group of palms, and on the other side we came upon our friend the fakir, who had again succeeded in spoiling our sport. The long, lanky figure was drawn to its full height, the white eyeballs and jagged teeth caught the red glint of the setting sun, and he waved his hand triumphantly in the direction of the vanishing cloud of birds.

Then there came the loud report of a gun, and the next thing I saw was a quivering body on the ground, and wild eyes staring open in the agony of death. Caulfield had shot the fakir, and now he stood looking down at what he had done, while I knelt beside the body and tried hopelessly to persuade myself that life was not extinct. When I got up we gazed at each other for a moment in silence.

'What are we to do?' I asked presently.

'Well, you know what it means,' Caulfield said in a queer, hard voice. 'Killing a native is no joke in these days, and I should come out of it pretty badly.'

I glanced at the body in horror. The face was rigid, and seemed more beast-like than ever. I looked at Caulfield again before I spoke, hesitatingly.

'Of course the whole thing was unpremeditated—an accident.'

'No, it wasn't,' he said defiantly, I meant to shoot the brute, and it served him right. And you can't say anything else if it comes out. But I don't see why anyone should know about it but ourselves.'

'It's nasty business,' I said, my heart sinking at the suggestion of concealment.

'It will be nastier still if we don't keep it dark, and you won't like having to give me away, you know. Either we must bury the thing here and say nothing about it, or else we must take it back to the station and stand the devil's own fuss. Probably I shall be kicked out of the service.'

'Of course I'll stand by you,' I said with an effort, 'but we can't do anything this minute. We'd better hide it in that long grass and come back after dinner. We must have something to dig with.'

Caulfield agreed sullenly, and between us we pushed the body in amongst the thick, coarse grass, which completely concealed it, and then made our way back to the camp. We ordered dinner and pretended to eat it, after which we sat for half an hour smoking, until the plates were cleared away and the servants had left the tent. Then I put my hunting-knife into my pocket, and Caulfield picked up a kitchen chopper that his bearer had left lying on the floor, after hammering a stiff joint of a camp chair, and we quitted the tent casually as though intending to have a stroll in the moonlight, which was almost as bright as day. We walked slowly at first, gradually increasing our pace as we left the camp behind us, and Caulfield never spoke a word until we came close to the tall grass that hid the fakir's body. Then he suddenly clutched my arm.

'God in heaven!' he whispered, pointing ahead, 'What is that?'

I saw the grass moving, and heard a scraping sound that made my heart stand still. We moved forward in desperation and parted the grass with our hands. A large jackal was lying on the fakir's body, grinning and snarling at being disturbed over his hideous meal.

'Drive it away,' said Caulfield, hoarsely. But the brute refused to move, and as it lay there showing its teeth, its face reminded me horribly of the wretched man dead beneath its feet. I turned sick and faint, so Caulfield shouted and shook the grass and threw clods of soil at the animal, which rose at last and slunk slowly away. It was an unusually large jackal, more like a wolf, and had lost one of its ears. The coat was rough, and mangy and thickly sprinkled with grey.

For more than an hour we worked desperately with the chopper and hunting-knife, being greatly aided in our task by a rift in the ground where the soil had been softened by water running from the jheel, and finally we stood up with the sweat pouring from our faces, and stamped down the earth which now covered all traces of Caulfield's crime. We had filled the grave with some large stones that were lying about (remnants of some ancient temple, long ago deserted and forgotten), thus feeling secure that it could not easily be disturbed by animals.

The next morning we returned to the station, and Caulfield shut himself up more than ever. He entirely dropped his shooting, which before had been his one pleasure, and the only person he ever spoke to, unofficially, was myself.

The end of April came with its plague of insects and scorching winds. The hours grew long and weary with the heat, and dust storms howled and swirled over the station, bringing perhaps a few tantalizing drops of rain, of more often leaving the air thick with a copper-coloured haze.

One night when it was too hot to sleep, Caulfield suddenly appeared in my verandah and asked me to let him stay the night in my bungalow.

'I know I'm an ass,' he said in awkward apology, 'but I can't stay by myself. I get all sorts of beastly ideas.'

I asked no questions, but gave him a cheroot and tried to cheer him up, telling him scraps of gossip, and encouraging him to talk, when a sound outside made us both start. It proved to be only the weird, plaintive cry of a jackal, but Caulfield sprang to his feet, shaking all over.

'There it is again!' he exclaimed. 'It has followed me over here. Listen!' turning his haggard, sleepless eyes on me. 'Every night that brute comes and howls round my house, and I tell you, on my oath, it's the same jackal we saw eating the poor devil I shot.'

'Nonsense, my dear chap,' I said, pushing him back into the chair, 'you must have got fever. Jackals come and howl round my house all night. That's nothing.'

'Look here,' said Caulfield, very calmly, 'I have no more fever than you have, and if you imagine I am delirious you are mistaken.' He lowered his voice. 'I looked out one night and saw the brute. It had only one ear!'

In spite of my own common sense and the certainty that Caulfield was not himself, my blood ran cold, and after I had succeeded in quieting him and he had dropped off to sleep on the couch, I sat in my long chair for hours, going over in my mind every detail of that horrible night in the jungle.

Several times after this Caulfield came to me and repeated the same tale. He swore he was being haunted by the jackal we had driven away from the fakir's body, and finally took it into his head that the spirit of the murdered man had entered the animal and was bent on obtaining vengeance.

Then he suddenly ceased coming over to me, and when I went to see him he would hardly speak, and only seemed anxious to get rid of me. I urged him to take leave or see a doctor, but he angrily refused to do either, and said he wished I would keep away from him altogether. So I left him alone for a couple of days, but on the third evening my conscience pricked me for having neglected him, and I was preparing to go over to his bungalow, when his bearer rushed in with a face of terror and besought me to come without delay. He said he feared his master was dying, and he had already sent for the doctor. The latter arrived in Caulfield's verandah simultaneously with myself, and together we entered the sick man's room. Caulfield was lying unconscious on his bed.

'He had a sort of fit, sahib,' said the frightened bearer, and proceeded to explain how his master had behaved.

The doctor bent over the bed.

'Do you happen to know if he had been bitten by a dog lately?' he asked, looking up at me.

'Not to my knowledge,' I answered, while the faint wail of a jackal out across the plain struck a chill to my heart.

For twenty-four hours we stayed with Caulfield, watching the terrible struggles we were powerless to relieve, and which lasted till the end came. He was never able to speak after the first paroxysm, which had occurred before we arrived, so we could not learn from him whether he had been bitten or not, neither could the doctor discover any scar on his body which might have been made by the teeth of an animal. Yet there was no shadow of doubt that Caulfield's death was due to hydrophobia.

As we stood in the next room when all was over, drinking the dead man's whisky and soda, which we badly needed, we questioned the bearer closely, but he could tell us little or nothing. His master, he said, did not keep dogs, nor had the bearer ever heard of his having been bitten by one; but there had been a mad jackal about the place nearly three weeks ago which his master had tried to shoot but failed.

'It couldn't have been that,' said the doctor, 'he would have come to me if he had been bitten by a jackal.'

'No,' I answered mechanically, 'it could not have been that.' And I went into the bedroom to take a last look at poor Caulfield's thin, white face with its ghastly, hunted expression, for there was now nothing more that I could do for him.

Then I picked up a lantern and stepped out into the dark verandah, intending to go home. As I did so, something came silently round the corner of the house and stood in my path. I raised my lantern and caught a glimpse of a mass of grey fur, two fiery yellow eyes, and bared, glistening teeth. It was only a stray jackal, and I struck at it with my stick, but instead of running away it slipped past me and entered Caulfield's room. The light fell on the animal's head, and I saw that it had only one ear.

In a frenzy I rushed back into the house calling for the doctor and servants.

'I saw a jackal come in here,' I said, searching round the bedroom, 'hunt it out at once.'

Every nook and corner was examined, but no jackal was found.

'Go home to bed, my boy, and keep quiet till I come and see you in the morning,' said the doctor, looking at me keenly. 'This business has shaken your nerves, and your imagination is beginning to play you tricks. Goodnight.' 'Goodnight,' I answered, and went slowly back to my bungalow, trying to persuade myself that he was right.

THE DOLL'S GHOST

F. Marion Crawford

It was a terrible accident, and for one moment the splendid machinery of Cranston House got out of gear and stood still. The butler emerged from the retirement in which he spent his elegant leisure, two grooms of the chambers appeared simultaneously from opposite directions, there were actually housemaids on the grand staircase, and those who remember the facts most exactly assert that Mrs Pringle herself positively stood upon the landing. Mrs Pringle was the housekeeper. As for the head nurse, the under nurse and the nursery-maid, their feelings cannot be described.

The Lady Gwendolen Lancaster-Douglas-Scroop, youngest daughter of the ninth Duke of Cranston, and aged six years and three months, picked herself up quite alone, and sat down on the third step of the grand staircase in Cranston House.

'Oh!' ejaculated the butler, and he disappeared again.

'Ah!' responded the grooms of the chambers, as they also went away.

'It's only that doll,' Mrs Pringle was distinctly heard to say, in a tone of contempt.

The under nurse heard her say it. Then the three nurses gathered round Lady Gwendolen and patted her, and gave her unhealthy things out of their pockets, and hurried her out of Cranston House as fast as they could, lest it should be found out upstairs that they had allowed the Lady Gwendolen Lancaster-

Douglas-Scroop to tumble down the grand staircase with her doll in her arms. And as the doll was badly broken, the nursery-maid carried it, with the pieces wrapped up in Lady Gwendolen's little cloak. It was not far to Hyde Park, and when they had reached a quiet place they took means to find out that Lady Gwendolen had no bruises. For the carpet was very thick and soft, and there was thick stuff under it to make it softer.

Lady Gwendolen Lancaster-Douglas-Scroop sometimes yelled, but she never cried. It was because she had yelled that the nurse had allowed her to go downstairs alone with Nina, the doll, under one arm, while she steadied herself with her other hand on the balustrade, and trod upon the polished marble steps beyond the edge of the carpet. So she had fallen, and Nina had come to grief.

◆

Mr Bernard Puckler and his little daughter lived in a little house in a little alley, which led out off a quiet little street not very far from Belgrave Square. He was the great doll doctor, and his extensive practice lay in the most aristocratic quarter. He mended dolls of all sizes and ages, boy dolls and girl dolls, baby dolls in long clothes, and grown-up dolls in fashionable gowns, talking dolls and dumb dolls, those that shut their eyes when they lay down, and those whose eyes had to be shut for them by means of a mysterious wire. His daughter Else was only just over twelve years old, but she was already very clever at mending dolls' clothes, and at doing their hair, which is harder than you might think, though the dolls sit quite still while it is being done.

Mr Puckler had originally been a German, but he had dissolved his nationality in the ocean of London many years ago, like a great many foreigners. He still had one or two German friends, however, who came on Saturday evenings and smoked with him and played picquet or 'skat' with him for farthing points, and called him 'Herr Doktor', which seemed to please Mr Puckler very much.

He looked older than he was, for his beard was rather long and ragged, his hair was grizzled and thin, and he wore horn-rimmed spectacles.

As for Else, she was a thin, pale child, very quiet and neat, with dark eyes and brown hair that was plaited down her back and tied with a bit of black ribbon. She mended the dolls' clothes and took the dolls back to their homes when they were quite strong again.

The house was a little one, but too big for the two people who lived in it. There was a small sitting-room on the street, and the workshop was at the back, and there were three rooms upstairs.

But the father and daughter lived most of their time in the workshop, because they were generally at work, even in the evenings.

Mr Puckler laid Nina on the table and looked at her a long time, till the tears began to fill his eyes behind the horn-rimmed spectacles. He was a very susceptible man, and he often fell in love with the dolls he mended, and found it hard to part with them when they had smiled at him for a few days. They were real little people to him, with characters and thoughts and feelings of their own, and he was very tender with them all. But some attracted him especially from the first, and when they were brought to him maimed and injured, their state seemed so pitiful to him that the tears came easily. You must remember that he had lived among dolls during a great part of his life, and understood them.

'How do you know that they feel nothing?' he went on to

say to Else. 'You must be gentle with them. It costs nothing to be kind to the little beings, and perhaps it makes a difference to them.'

And Else understood him, because she was a child, and she knew that she was more to him than all the dolls.

He fell in love with Nina at first sight, perhaps because her beautiful brown glass eyes were something like Else's own, and he loved Else first and best, with all his heart. And, besides, it was a very sorrowful case. Nina had evidently not been long in the world, for her complexion was perfect, her hair was smooth where it should be smooth, and curly where it should be curly, and her silk clothes were perfectly new. But across her face was that frightful gash, like a sabre-cut, deep and shadowy within, but clean and sharp at the edges. When he tenderly pressed her head to close the gaping wound, the edges made a fine, grating sound, that was painful to hear, and the lids of the dark eyes quivered and trembled as though Nina were suffering dreadfully.

'Poor Nina!' he exclaimed sorrowfully. 'But I shall not hurt you much, though you will take a long time to get strong.'

He always asked the names of the broken dolls when they were brought to him, and sometimes the people knew what the children called them, and told him. He liked 'Nina' for a name. Altogether and in every way she pleased him more than any doll he had seen for many years, and he felt drawn to her, and made up his mind to make her perfectly strong and sound, no matter how much labour it might cost him.

Mr Puckler worked patiently a little at a time, and Else watched him. She could do nothing for poor Nina, whose clothes needed no mending. The longer the doll doctor worked the more fond he became of the yellow hair and the beautiful brown glass eyes. He sometimes forgot all the other dolls that were waiting to be mended, lying side by side on a shelf, and sat for an hour gazing at Nina's face, while he racked his ingenuity for some new invention by which to hide even the smallest trace of the terrible accident.

She was wonderfully mended. Even he was obliged to admit that; but the scar was still visible to his keen eyes, a very fine line right across the face, downwards from right to left. Yet all the conditions had been most favourable for a cure, since the cement had set quite hard at the first attempt and the weather had been fine and dry, which makes a great difference in a dolls' hospital. At last he knew that he could do no more, and the under nurse had already come twice to see whether the job was finished, as she coarsely expressed it.

'Nina is not quite strong yet,' Mr Puckler had answered each time, for he could not make up his mind to face the parting.

And now he sat before the square deal table at which he worked, and Nina lay before him for the last time with a big brown-paper box beside her. It stood there like her coffin, waiting for her, he thought. He must put her into it, and lay tissue paper over her dear face, and then put on the lid, and at the thought of tying the string his sight was dim with tears again. He was never to look into the glassy depths of the beautiful brown eyes any more, nor to hear the little wooden voice say 'Pa-pa' and 'Ma-ma'. It was a very painful moment.

In the vain hope of gaining time before the separation, he took up the little sticky bottles of cement and glue and gum and colour, looking at each one in turn, and then at Nina's face. And all his small tools lay there, neatly arranged in a row, but he knew that he could not use them again for Nina. She was quite strong at last, and in a country where there should be no cruel children to hurt her she might live a hundred years, with only that almost imperceptible line across her face, to tell of the fearful thing that had befallen her on the marble steps of Cranston House.

Suddenly Mr Puckler's heart was quite full, and he rose abruptly from his seat and turned away.

'Else,' he said unsteadily, 'you must do it for me. I cannot bear to see her go into the box.'

So he went and stood at the window with his back turned, while Else did what he had not the heart to do.

'Is it done?' he asked, not turning round. 'Then take her away, my dear. Put on your hat, and take her to Cranston House quickly, and when you are gone I will turn round.'

Else was used to her father's queer ways with the dolls, and though she had never seen him so much moved by a parting, she was not much surprised.

'Come back quickly,' he said, when he heard her hand on the latch. 'It is growing late, and I should not send you at this hour. But I cannot bear to look forward to it any more.'

When Else was gone, he left the window and sat down in his place before the table again, to wait for the child to come back, He touched the place where Nina had lain, very gently, and he recalled the softly-tinted pink face, and the glass eyes, and the ringlets of yellow hair, till he could almost see them.

The evenings wore long, for it was late in the spring. But it began to grow dark soon, and Mr Puckler wondered why Else did not come back. She had been gone an hour and a half, and that was much longer than he had expected, for it was barely half a mile from Belgrave Square to Cranston House. He reflected that the child might have been kept waiting, but as the twilight deepened he grew anxious, and walked up and down in the dim workshop, no longer thinking of Nina, but of Else, his own living child, whom he loved.

An indefinable, disquieting sensation came upon him by fine degrees, a chilliness and a faint stirring of his thin hair, joined with a wish to be in any company rather than to be alone much longer. It was the beginning of fear.

He told himself in strong German-English that he was a foolish old man, and he began to feel about for the matches in the dusk. He knew just where they should be, for he always kept them in the same place, close to the little tin box that held bits of sealing wax of various colours, for some kinds of mending. But somehow he could not find the matches in the gloom.

Something had happened to Else, he was sure, and as his fear increased, he felt as though it might be allayed if he could get a light and see what time it was. Then he called himself a foolish old man again, and the sound of his own voice startled him in the dark. He could not find the matches.

The window was grey still; he might see what time it was if he went close to it, and he could go and get matches out of the cupboard afterwards. He stood back from the table, to get out of the way of the chair, and began to cross the board floor.

Something was following him in the dark. There was a small pattering, as of tiny feet upon the boards. He stopped and listened, and the roots of his hair tingled. It was nothing and he was a foolish old man. He made two steps more, and he was sure that he heard the little pattering again. He turned his back to the window, leaning against the sash so that the panes began to crack, and he faced the dark. Everything was quite still, and it smelt of paste and cement and wood-filings as usual.

'Is that you, Else?' he asked, and he was surprised by the fear in his voice.

There was no answer in the room, and he held up his watch and tried to make out what time it was by the grey dusk that was just not darkness. So far as he could see, it was within two or three minutes of ten o'clock. He had been a long time alone. He was shocked and frightened for Else, out in London, so late, and he almost ran across the room to the door. As he fumbled for the latch, he distinctly heard the running of the little feet after him.

'Mice!' he exclaimed feebly, just as he got the door open.

He shut it quickly behind him, and felt as though some cold thing had settled on his back and was writhing upon him. The passage was quite dark, but he found his hat and was out in the alley in a moment, breathing more freely, and surprised to find how much light there still was in the open air. He could see the pavement clearly under his feet, and far off in the street to which the alley led he could hear the laughter and calls of children, playing some game out of doors. He wondered how he could have been so nervous, and for an instant he thought of going back into the house to wait quietly for Else. But instantly he felt that nervous fright of something stealing over him again. In any case it was better to walk up to Cranston House and ask the servants about the child. One of the women had perhaps taken a fancy to her, and was even now giving her tea and cake.

He walked quickly to Belgrave Square, and then up the broad streets, listening as he went, whenever there was no other sound, for the tiny footsteps. But he heard nothing, and was laughing at himself when he rang the servants' bell at the big house. Of course, the child must be there.

The person who opened the door was quite an inferior person—for it was a back door—but affected the manners of the front, and stared at Mr Puckler superciliously.

No little girl had been seen, and he knew 'nothing about no dolls'.

'She is my little girl,' said Mr Puckler tremulously, for all his anxiety was returning tenfold, 'and I am afraid something has happened.'

The inferior person said rudely that 'nothing could have

happened to her in that house, because she had not been there, which was a jolly good reason why'; and Mr Puckler was obliged to admit that the man ought to know, as it was his business to keep the door and let people in. He wished to be allowed to speak to the under nurse, who knew him; but the man was ruder than ever, and finally shut the door in his face.

When the doll doctor was alone in the street, he steadied himself by the railing, for he felt as though he were breaking in two, just as some dolls break, in the middle of the backbone.

Presently he knew that he must be doing something to find Else, and that gave him strength. He began to walk as quickly as he could through the streets, following every highway and byway which his little girl might have taken on her errand. He also asked several policemen in vain if they had seen her, and most of them answered him kindly, for they saw that he was a sober man and in his right senses, and some of them had little girls of their own.

It was one o'clock in the morning when he went up to his own door again, worn out and hopeless and broken-hearted. As he turned the key in the lock, his heart stood still, for he knew that he was awake and not dreaming, and that he really heard those tiny footsteps pattering to meet him inside the house along the passage.

But he was too unhappy to be much frightened anymore, and his heart went on again with a dull regular pain, that found its way all through him with every pulse. So he went in, and hung up his hat in the dark, and found the matches in the cupboard and the candlestick in its place in the corner. Mr Puckler was so much overcome and so completely worn out that he sat down in his chair before the work-table and almost fainted, as his face dropped forward upon his folded hands. Beside him the solitary candle burned steadily with a low flame in the still warm air.

'Else! Else!' he moaned against his yellow knuckles. And that was all he could say, and it was no relief to him. On the contrary, the very sound of the name was a new and sharp pain that pierced his ears and his head and his very soul. For every time he repeated the name it meant that little Else was dead, somewhere out in the streets of London in the dark.

He was so terribly hurt that he did not even feel something pulling gently at the skirt of his old coat, so gently that it was like the nibbling of a tiny mouse. He might have thought that it was really a mouse if he had noticed it.

'Else! Else!' he groaned, right against his hands.

Then a cool breath stirred his thin hair, and the low flame of the one candle dropped down almost to a mere spark, not flickering, as though a draught were going to blow it out, but just dropping down as if it were tired out. Mr Puckler felt his hands stiffening with fright under his face; and there was a faint rustling sound, like some small silk thing blown in a gentle breeze. He sat up straight, stark and scared, and a small wooden voice spoke in the stillness.

'Pa-pa,' it said, with a break between the syllables.

Mr Puckler stood up in a single jump, and his chair fell over backwards with a smashing noise upon the wooden floor. The candle had almost gone out.

It was Nina's doll-voice that had spoken, and he should have known it among the voices of a hundred other dolls. And yet there was something more in it, a little human ring, with a pitiful cry and a call for help, and the wail of a hurt child. Mr Puckler stood up, stark and stiff, and tried to look round, but at first he could not, for he seemed to be frozen from head to foot.

Then he made a great effort, and he raised one hand to each of his temples, and pressed his own head round as he would have turned a doll's. The candle was burning so low that it might as well have been out altogether, for any light it gave, and the room seemed quite dark at first. Then he saw something. He would not have believed that he could be more frightened than he had been just before that. But he was, and his knees shook, for he saw the doll standing in the middle of the floor, shining with a faint and ghostly radiance, her beautiful glassy brown eyes fixed on his. And across her face the very thin line of the break he had mended shone as though it were drawn in light with a line point of white flame.

Yet there was something more in the eyes, too; there was something human, like Else's own, but as if only the doll saw him through them, and not Else. And there was enough of Else to bring back all his pain and to make him forget his fear.

'Else! My little Else!' he cried aloud.

The small ghost moved, and its doll-arm slowly rose and fell with a stiff,' mechanical motion.

'Pa-pa,' it said.

It seemed this time that there was even more of Else's tone echoing somewhere between the wooden notes that reached his ears so distinctly and yet so far away. Else was calling him, he was sure. His face was perfectly white in the gloom, but his knees did not shake any more, and he felt that he was less frightened.

'Yes, child! But where? Where?' he asked. 'Where are you, Else?'

'Pa-pa!'

The syllables died away in the quiet room.

There was a low rustling of silk, the glassy brown eyes turned slowly away, and Mr Puckler heard the pitter-patter of the small feet in the bronze kid slippers as the figure ran straight to the door. Then the candle burned high again, the room was full of light, and he was alone.

Mr Puckler passed his hand over his eyes and looked about him. He could see everything quite clearly, and he felt that he must have been dreaming, though he was standing instead of sitting down, as he should have been if he had just waked up. The candle burned brightly now. There were the dolls to be mended, lying in a row with their toes up. The third one had lost her right shoe, and Else was making one. He knew that, and he was certainly not dreaming now. He had not been dreaming when he had come in from his fruitless search and had heard the doll's footsteps running to the door. He had not fallen asleep in his chair. How could he possibly have fallen asleep when his heart was breaking? He had been awake all the time.

He steadied himself, set the fallen chair upon its legs, and said to himself again very emphatically that he was a foolish old man. He ought to be out in the streets looking for his child, asking questions, and enquiring at the police stations where all accidents were reported as soon as they were known, or at the hospitals.

'Pa-pa!'

The longing, wailing, pitiful little wooden cry rang from the passage, outside the door, and Mr Puckler stood for an instant with white face, transfixed and rooted to the spot. A moment later his hand was on the latch. Then he was in the passage, with the light streaming from the open door behind him.

Quite at the other end he saw the little phantom shining clearly in the shadow, and the right hand seemed to beckon to him as the arm rose and fell once more. He knew all at once that it had not come to frighten him but to lead him, and when it disappeared, and he walked boldly towards the door, he knew that it was in the street outside, waiting for him. He forgot that he was tired and had eaten no supper, and had walked many miles, for a sudden hope ran through and through him, like a golden stream of life.

And sure enough, at the corner of the alley, and at the corner of the street, and out in Belgrave Square, he saw the small ghost flitting before him. Sometimes it was only a shadow, where there was other light, but then the glare of the lamps made a pale green sheen on its little Mother Hubbard frock of silk; and sometimes, where the streets were dark and silent, the whole figure shone out brightly with its yellow curls and rosy neck. It seemed to trot along like a tiny child, and Mr Puckler could hear the pattering of the bronze kid slippers on the pavement as it ran. But it went very fast, and he could only just keep up with it, tearing along with his hat on the back of his head and his thin hair blown by the night breeze, and his horn-rimmed spectacles firmly set upon his broad nose.

On and on he went, and he had no idea where he was. He did not even care, for he knew certainly that he was going the right way.

Then at last, in a wide, quiet street, he was standing before a big, sober-looking door that had two lamps on each side of it, and a polished brass bell-handle, which he pulled.

And just inside, when the door was opened, in the bright light, there was the little shadow, and the pale green sheen of the little silk dress, and once more the small cry came to his ears, less pitiful, more longing.

'Pa-pa!'

The shadow turned suddenly bright, and out of the brightness the beautiful brown glass eyes were turned up happily to his, while the rosy mouth smiled so divinely that the phantom doll looked almost like a little angel just then.

'A little girl was brought in soon after ten o'clock,' said the quiet voice of the hospital doorkeeper. 'I think they thought she was only stunned. She was holding a big brown-paper box against her, and they could not get it out of her arms. She had a long plait of brown hair that hung down as they carried her.'

'She is my little girl,' said Mr Puckler, but he hardly heard his own voice.

He leaned over Else's face in the gentle light of the children's ward, and when he had stood there a minute the beautiful brown eyes opened and looked up to his.

'Pa-pa!' cried Else softly, 'I knew you would come!'

Then Mr Puckler did not know what he did or said for a moment, and what he felt was worth all the fear and terror and despair that had almost killed him that night. But by and by Else was telling her story, and the nurse let her speak, for there were only two other children in the room, who were getting well and were sound asleep.

'They were big boys with bad faces,' said Else, 'and they tried to get Nina away from me, but I held on and fought as well as I could till one of them hit me with something, and I don't remember any more, for I tumbled down and I suppose the boys ran away, and somebody found me there. But I'm afraid Nina is all smashed.'

'Here is the box,' said the nurse. 'We could not take it out of her arms till she came to herself. Would you like to see if the doll is broken?'

And she undid the string cleverly, but Nina was all smashed to pieces. Only the gentle light of the children's ward made a pale green sheen in the folds of the little Mother Hubbard frock.

THEY NEVER GET CAUGHT

Margery Allingham

The murder was planned carefully, patiently, and carried out without any fuss. The only person who was really disconcerted was the victim. The queen of crime writing at her best...

'*Millie dear, this does explain itself, doesn't it? Henry.*' Mr Henry Brownrigg signed his name on the back of the little blue bill with a flourish. Then he set the scrap of paper carefully in the exact centre of the imperfectly scoured developing bath, and, leaving the offending utensil on the kitchen table for his wife to find when she came in, he stalked back to the shop, feeling that he had administered the rebuke surely and at the same time gracefully.

In fifteen years Mr Brownrigg felt that he had mastered the art of teaching his wife her job. Not that he had taught her. That, Mr Brownrigg felt, with a woman of Millie's staggering obtuseness was past praying for. But now, after long practice, he could deliver the snub or administer the punishing word in a way which would penetrate her placid dullness.

Within half an hour after she had returned from shopping and before lunch was set upon the table, he knew the bath would be back in the dark-room, bright and pristine as when it was new, and nothing more would be said about it. Millie would be a little more ineffectually anxious to please at lunch, perhaps, but that was all.

Mr Brownrigg passed behind the counter and flicked a speck of dust off the dummy cartons of face-cream. It was 12.25 and a half. In four and a half minutes Phyllis Bell would leave her office further down the High Street, and in seven and a half minutes she would come in through that narrow, sunlit doorway to the cool, drug-scented shop.

On that patch of floor where the sunlight lay blue and yellow, since it had found its way in through the enormous glass vases in the window which were the emblem of his trade, she would stand and look at him, her blue eyes limpid and her small mouth pursed and adorable.

The chemist took up one of the ebony-backed hand mirrors exposed on the counter for sale and glanced at himself in it. He was not altogether a prepossessing person. Never a tall man, at forty-two his wide, stocky figure showed a definite tendency to become fleshy, but there was strength and virility in his thick shoulders, while his clean-shaven face and broad neck were short and bull-like and his lips were full.

Phyllis liked his eyes. They held her, she said, and most of the other young women who bought their cosmetics at the corner shop and chatted with Mr Brownrigg across the counter might have been inclined to agree with her.

Over-dark, round, hot eyes had Mr Brownrigg; not at all the sort of eyes for a little, plump, middle-aged chemist with a placid wife like Millie.

But Mr Brownrigg did not contemplate his own eyes. He smoothed his hair, wiped his lips, and then, realizing that Phyllis was almost due, he disappeared behind the dispensing desk. It was as well, he always thought, not to appear too eager.

He was watching the door, though, when she came in. He saw the flicker of her green skirt as she hesitated on the step and saw her half eager, half apprehensive expression as she glanced towards the counter.

He was glad she had not come in when a customer was there. Phyllis was different from any of the others whose little histories stretched back through the past fourteen years. When Phyllis was in the shop Mr Brownrigg found he was liable to make mistakes, liable to drop things and fluff the change.

He came out from his obscurity eager in spite of himself, and drew the little golden-haired girl sharply towards him over that part of the counter which was lowest and which he purposely kept uncluttered.

He kissed her and the sudden hungry force of the movement betrayed him utterly. He heard her quick intake of breath before she released herself and stepped back.

'You—you shouldn't,' she said, nervously tugging her hat back into position.

She was barely twenty, small and young looking for her years, with yellow hair and a pleasant, quiet style. Her blue eyes were frightened and a little disgusted now, as though she found herself caught up in an emotion which her instincts considered not quite nice.

Henry Brownrigg recognized the expression. He had seen it before in other eyes, but whereas on past occasions he had been able to be tolerantly amused and therefore comforting and glibly reassuring, in Phyllis it irritated and almost frightened him.

'Why not?' he demanded sharply, too sharply he knew immediately, and the blood rushed into his face.

Phyllis took a deep breath.

'I came to tell you,' she said jerkily, like a child saying its piece, 'I've been thinking things over. I can't go on with all this. You're married. I want to be married some day. I—I shan't come in again.'

'You haven't been talking to someone?' he demanded, suddenly cold.

'About you? Good heavens, no!'

Her vehemence was convincing, and because of that he shut his mind to its uncomplimentary inference and experienced only relief

'You love me,' said Henry Brownrigg. 'I love you and you love me. You know that.'

He spoke without intentional histrionics, but adopted a curious monotone which, some actors have discovered, is one of the most convincing methods of conveying deep sincerity.

Phyllis nodded miserably and then seemed oddly embarrassed. Wistfully her eyes wandered to the sunlit street and back again.

'Goodbye,' she said huskily and fled.

He saw her speeding past the window, almost running.

For some time Henry Brownrigg remained looking down at the patch of blue sunlight where she had stood. Finally he raised his eyes and smiled with conscious wryness. She would come back. Tomorrow, or in a week, or in ten days perhaps, she would come back. But the obstacle, the insurmountable obstacle would arise again, in time it would defeat him and he would lose her.

Phyllis was different from the others. He would lose her. Unless that obstacle were removed.

Henry Brownrigg frowned.

There were other considerations too. The old, mottled ledger told those only too clearly.

If the obstacle were removed it would automatically wipe away those difficulties also, for was there not the insurance and that small income Millie's father had left so securely tied, as though the old man had divined his daughter would grow up a fool?

Mr Brownrigg's eyes rested upon the little drawer under the counter marked: 'Prescriptions: private.' It was locked and not even young Perry, his errand boy and general assistant, who poked his nose into most things, guessed that under the pile of slips within was a packet of letters scrawled in Phyllis's childish hand.

He turned away abruptly. His breath was hard to draw and he was trembling. The time had come.

Some months previously Henry Brownrigg had decided that he must become a widower before the end of the year, but the interview of the morning had convinced him that he must hurry.

At this moment Millie, her face still pink with shame at the recollection of the affair of the ill-washed bath, put her head round the inner door.

'Lunch is on the table, Henry,' she said, and added with that stupidity which had annoyed him ever since it had ceased to please him by making him feel superior. 'Well, you do look serious. Oh, Henry, you haven't made a mistake and given somebody a wrong bottle?'

'No, my dear Millie,' said her husband, surveying her coldly and speaking with heavy sarcasm. 'That is the peculiar sort of idiot mistake I have yet to make. I haven't reached my wife's level yet.'

And as he followed her uncomplaining figure to the little room behind the shop a word echoed rhythmically in the back of his mind and kept time with the beating of his heart. 'Hurry! Hurry! Hurry!'

'Henry, dear,' said Millie Brownrigg, turning a troubled face towards her husband, 'why Doctor Crupiner? He's so expensive and so old.'

She was standing in front of the dressing-table in the big

front bedroom above the shop, brushing her brown, grey streaked hair before she plaited it and coiled it round her head.

Henry Brownrigg, lying awake in his bed on the far side of the room, did not answer her.

Millie went on talking. She was used to Henry's silence. Henry was so clever. Most of his time was spent in thought.

'I've heard all sorts of odd things about Doctor Crupiner,' she remarked. 'They say he's so old he forgets. Why shouldn't we go to Mother's man? She swears by him.'

'Unfortunately for your mother she has your intelligence, without a man to look after her, poor woman,' said Henry Brownrigg.

Millie made no comment.

'Crupiner,' continued Henry Brownrigg, 'may not be much good as a general practitioner, but there is one subject on which he is a master. I want him to see you. I want to get you well, old dear.'

Millie's gentle, expressionless face flushed and her blue eyes looked moist and foolish in the mirror. Henry could see her reflection in the glass and he turned away. There were moments when, by her obvious gratitude for a kind word from him, Millie made him feel a certain distaste for his project. He wished to God she would go away and leave him his last few moments in bed to think of Phyllis in peace.

'You know, Henry,' said Mrs Brownrigg suddenly, 'I don't feel ill. Those things you're giving me are doing me good, I'm sure, I don't feel nearly so tired at the end of the day now. Can't you treat me yourself.'

The man in the bed stiffened. Any compunction he may have felt vanished and he became wary.

'Of course they're doing you good,' he said with the satisfaction of knowing that he was telling the truth up to a point, or at least of knowing that he was doing nothing reprehensible—yet.

'I don't believe in patent medicines as a rule, but Fender's pills are good. They're a well-known formula, and they certainly do pick one up. But I just want to make sure that you're organically sound. I don't like you getting breathless when you hurry, and the colour of your lips isn't good, you know.'

Plump, foolish Millie looked in the mirror and nervously ran her forefinger over her mouth.

Like many women of her age she had lost much of her colour, and there certainly was a faint, very faint, blue streak round the edge of her lips.

The Chemist was heavily reassuring.

'Nothing to worry about, I'm sure, but I think we'll go down and see Crupiner this evening,' he said, and added adroitly, 'we want to be on the safe side, don't we?'

Millie nodded, her mouth trembling.

'Yes, dear,' she said, and paused, adding afterwards in that insufferable way of hers, 'I suppose so.'

When she had gone downstairs to attend to breakfast Henry Brownrigg rose with his own last phrase still on his lips. He repeated it thoughtfully.

'The safe side.' That was right. The safe side. No ghastly hash of it for Henry Brownrigg.

Only fools made a hash of things. Only fools got caught. This was almost too easy. Millie was so simple-minded, so utterly unsuspecting.

By the end of the day Mr Brownrigg was nervy. The boy Perry had reported innocently enough that he had seen young Hill in his new car going down Acacia Road at something over sixty, and had added casually that he had had the Bell girl with him. The youngest one. Phyllis. Did Mr Brownrigg remember her? She was rather pretty.

For a moment Henry Brownrigg was in terror lest the boy had discovered his secret and was wounding him maliciously. But, having convinced himself that this was not so, the fact and the sting remained.

Young Hill was handsome and a bachelor. Phyllis was young and impressionable. The Chemist imagined them pulling up in some shady copse outside the town, holding hands, perhaps even kissing, and the heart which could remain steady while Millie's stupid eyes met his anxiously as she spoke of her illness turned over painfully in Henry Brownrigg's side at the thought of that embrace.

'Hurry.' The word formed itself again in the back of his mind. Hurry...hurry.

Millie was breathless when they arrived at Doctor Crupiner's old-fashioned house. Henry had been self-absorbed and had walked very fast.

Doctor Crupiner saw them immediately. He was a vast, dusty old man. Privately Millie thought she would like to take a good stiff broom to him, and the picture the idea conjured in her mind was so ridiculous that she giggled nervously and Henry had to shake his head at her warningly.

She flushed painfully, and the old, stupid expression settled down over her face again.

Henry explained her symptoms to the doctor and Millie looked surprised and gratified at the anxiety he betrayed. Henry had evidently noticed her little wearinesses much more often than she had supposed.

When he had finished his recital of her small ills, none of them alarming in themselves but piling up in total to a rather terrifying sum of evidence, Doctor Crupiner turned his eyes, which were small and greasy, with red veins in their whites, on to Millie, and his old lips, which were mottled like Henry's ledger, moved for a fraction of a second before his voice came, wheezy and sepulchral.

'Well, madam,' he said, 'your husband here seems worried about you. Let's have a look at you.'

Millie trembled. She was getting breathless again from sheer apprehension. Once or twice lately it had occurred to her that the Fender's pills made her feel breathless, even while they bucked her up in other ways, but she had not liked to mention this to Henry.

Doctor Crupiner came close to her, breathing heavily through his nose in an effort of concentration. He thrust a stubby, unsteady finger into her eye socket, dragging down the skin so that he could peer short-sightedly at her eyeball. He thumped her half-heartedly on the back and felt the palms of her hands.

Mr Brownrigg, who watched all this somewhat meaningless ritual, his round eyes thoughtful and uneasy, suddenly took the doctor on one side, and the two men had a muttered conversation at the far end of the long room.

Millie could not help overhearing some of it, because Doctor Crupiner was deaf these days and Henry was anxious to make himself understood.

'Twenty years ago,' she heard. 'Very sudden.' And then, after a pause, the awful word 'hereditary'.

Millie's trembling fit increased in intensity and her broad, stupid face looked frightened. They were talking about her poor Papa. He had died very suddenly of heart disease.

Her own heart jumped painfully. So that was why Henry seemed so anxious.

Doctor Crupiner came back to her. She had to undo her dress and Doctor Crupiner listened to her heart with an ancient stethoscope. Millie, already trembling, began to breathe with difficulty as her alarm became unbearable.

At last the old man finished with her. He stared at her unwinkingly for some seconds and finally turned to Henry, and together they went back to the far end of the room.

Millie strained her ears and heard the old man's rumbling voice.

'A certain irregularity. Nothing very alarming. Bring her to see me again.'

Then there was a question from Henry which she could not catch, but afterwards, as the doctor seemed to be fumbling in his mind for a reply, the Chemist remarked in an ordinary tone: 'I've been giving her Fender's pills.'

'Fender's pills?' Doctor Crupiner echoed the words with relief. 'Excellent. Excellent. You chemists like patent medicines, I know, and I don't want to encourage you, but that's a well-known formula and will save you mixing up my prescription. Carry on with those for a while. Very good things; I often recommend them. Take them in moderation, of course.'

'Oh, of course,' said Henry. 'But do you think I'm doing right, Doctor?'

Millie looked pleased and startled at the earnestness of Henry's tone.

'Oh, without doubt, Mr Brownrigg, without doubt,' Doctor Crupiner repeated the words again as he came back to Millie. 'There, Mrs Brownrigg,' he said with spurious jollity, 'you take care of yourself and do what your husband says. Come to see me again in a week or so and you'll be as right as ninepence. Off you go. Oh, but Mrs Brownrigg, no shocks, mind. No excitements. No little upsets. And don't over-tire yourself.'

He shook hands perfunctorily, and, while Henry was helping Millie to collect her things with a solicitude quite unusual in him, the old man took down a large, dusty book from the shelves.

Just before they left he peered at Henry over his spectacles.

'Those Fender's pills are quite a good idea,' he remarked in a tone quite different from his professional rumble. 'Just the things. They contain a small percentage of digitalin.'

◆

One of Mr Brownrigg's least attractive habits was his method of spending Saturday nights.

At half-past seven the patient but silently disapproving Millie would clear away the remains of the final meal of the day and place one glass and an unopened bottle of whisky and a siphon of soda on the green serge tablecloth.

This done, she would retire to the kitchen, wash up, and complete the week's ironing. She usually left this job until then, because it was a longish business, with frequent pauses for minor repairs to Henry's shirts and her own underclothing, and she knew she had plenty of undisturbed time on her hands.

She had, in fact, until midnight. When the kitchen clock wheezed twelve, Millie folded her ironing board and turned up the irons on thc stove to cool.

The she went into the living-room and took away the glass and the empty bottle, so that the daily help should not see them in the morning. She also picked up the papers and straightened the room.

Finally, when the gas fire had been extinguished, she attended to Henry.

A fortnight and three days after her first visit to Doctor Crupiner—the Doctor, at Henry's suggestion, had increased her dose of Fender's pills from three to five a day—she went through her Saturday ritual as usual.

For a man engaged in Mr Brownrigg's particular programme

to get hopelessly and incapably drunk once, much less once a week, might well have been suicidal lunacy.

One small glass of whisky reduced him to taciturnity. Twelve large glasses of whisky, or one bottle, made of him a limp, silent sack of humanity, incapable of movement or speech, but, quite remarkably, not a senseless creature.

It might well have occurred to Millie to wonder why her husband should chose to transform himself into a Therese Raquin paralytic once every week in his life, but in spite of her awful stupidity she was a tolerant woman and honestly believed that men were odd, privileged creatures who took delight in strange perversions. So she humoured him and kept his weakness secret even from her mother.

Oddly enough, Henry Brownrigg enjoyed his periodical orgy. He did not drink during the week, and his Saturday experience was at once an adventure and a habit. At the outset of his present project he had thought of foregoing it until his plan was completed, but he realised the absolute necessity of adhering rigidly to his normal course of life, so that there could be no hook, however small, on which the garment of suspicion could catch and take hold.

On this particular evening Millie quite exhausted herself getting him upstairs and into bed. She was so tired when it was all over that she sat on the edge of her couch and breathed hard, quite unable to pull herself together sufficiently to undress.

So exhausted was she that she forgot to take the two Fender's pills that Henry had left on the dressing-table for her, and once in bed she could not persuade herself to get out again for them.

In the morning Henry found them still in the little box. He listened to her startled explanations in silence and then, as she added apology to apology, suddenly became himself again.

'Dear Millie,' he said in the old exasperated tone she knew

so well, 'isn't it enough for me to do all I can to get you well without you hampering me at every turn?'

Millie bent low over the stove and, as if he felt she might be hiding sudden tears, his manner became more conciliatory.

'Don't you like them?' he inquired softly. 'Don't you like the taste of them? Perhaps they're too big? Look here, old dear, I'll put them up in an easier form. You shall have them in jelly cases. Leave it to me. There, there, don't worry. But you must take your medicine, you know.'

He patted her plump shoulder awkwardly and hurried upstairs to dress.

Millie became thoughtful. Henry was clearly very worried about her indeed, or he would never be so nice about her silly mistake.

◆

Young Bill Perry, Brownrigg's errand boy assistant, was at the awkward stage, if indeed he would ever grow out of it.

He was scrawny, red-headed, with a tendency to acne, and great raw, scarlet wrists. Mr Brownrigg he loathed as only the young can loathe the possessor of a sarcastic tongue, but Millie he liked, and his pale, sandy-fringed eyes twinkled kindly when she spoke to him.

Young Perry did not think Millie was half so daft as the Old Man made out.

If only because she was kind to him, young Perry was interested in the state of Millie's health.

On the Monday night young Perry saw Mr Brownrigg putting up the contents of the Fender's pills in jelly cases and he inquired about them.

Mr Brownrigg was unusually communicative. He told young Perry in strict confidence that Mrs Brownrigg was far from well and that Doctor Crupiner was worried about her.

Mr Brownrigg also intimated that he and Doctor Crupiner were, as professional men, agreed that if complete freedom from care and Fender's pills could not save Mrs Brownrigg, nothing could.

'Do you means she might die?' said young Perry, aghast. 'suddenly, I mean, Sir?'

He was sorry as soon as he had spoken, because Mr Brownrigg's hand trembled so much that he dropped one of the jelly cases and young Perry realized that the Old Man was really wild about the Old Girl after all, and that his bullyragging her was all a sham to hide his feelings.

At that moment young Perry's sentimental, impressionable heart went out to Mr Brownrigg, and he generously forgave him for his observation that young Perry was patently cut out for the diplomatic service, since his tact and delicacy were so great.

The stores arrived. Bill Perry unpacked the two big cases; the smaller case he opened, but left the unpacking to his employer.

Mr Brownrigg finished his pill making, although he was keeping the boy waiting, rinsed his hands and got down to work with his usual deliberation.

There were not a great many packages in the case and young Perry, who had taken a peep at the mottled ledger some time before, thought he knew why. The Old Man was riding close to the edge. Bills and receipts had to be juggled very carefully these days.

The boy read the invoice from the wholesaler's, and Mr Brownrigg put the drugs away.

'Sodii Bicarbonas, Magnesia Levis,' he read, stumbling over the difficult words. 'Iodine, Quininae Hydrochloridum, Tincture Digitalin…that must be it, Mr Brownrigg. There, in the biggish packet.'

Bill Perry knew he read badly and was only trying to be helpful when he indicated the parcel, but Mr Brownrigg shot a truly terrifying glance in his direction as he literally snatched up the package and carried it off to the drug cabinet.

Young Perry was dismayed. He was late and he wanted to go. In his panic he floundered on, making matters worse.

'I'm sorry, sir,' he said. 'I was only trying to help. I thought you might be—err—thinking of something else and got a bit muddled.'

'Oh,' said Mr Brownrigg slowly, fixing him with those hot, round eyes in a way which was oddly disturbing. 'And of what should I be thinking when I am doing my work, boy?'

'Of—of Mrs Brownrigg, Sir,' stammered the wretched Perry helplessly.

Henry Brownrigg froze. The blood congealed in his face and his eyes seemed to sink into his head.

Young Perry, who realized he had said the wrong thing, and who had a natural delicacy which revolted at prying into another's sorrow, mistook his employer's symptoms for acute embarrassment.

'I'm sorry,' he said again. 'I was really trying to help. I'm a bit—err—windy myself, Sir. Mrs Brownrigg's been very kind to be. I'm sorry she's so ill.'

A great sigh escaped Henry Brownrigg.

'That's all right, my boy,' he said, with a gentleness his assistant had never before heard in his tone. 'I'm a bit rattled myself, too. You can go now. I'll see to these few things.'

Young Perry sped off, happy to be free on such a sunny evening, but also a little awe-stricken by the revelation of this tragedy of married love.

Phylis hurried clown Coe's Lane, which was a short cut between her own road and Priory Avenue. It was a narrow, paper-baggy little thoroughfare, with a dusty hedge on one side and high tarred fence on the other.

On this occasion Coe's Lane appeared to be deserted, but when Phyllis reached the stunted may tree halfway down the hedge a figure stepped out and came to meet her.

The girl stopped abruptly in the middle of the path. Her cheeks were patched with pink and white and she caught her breath sharply as though afraid of herself.

Henry Brownrigg himself was unprepared for the savagery of the sudden pain in his breast when he saw her, and the writhing, vicious, mindless passion which checked his breathing and made his eyelids feel sticky and his mouth dry, frightened him a little also.

They were alone in the lane and he kissed her, putting into his hunched shoulders and greedy lips all the insufferable, senseless longing of the past eighteen days.

When he released her she was crying. The big, bright tears which filled her eyes brimmed over on to her cheeks and made her mouth look hot and wet and feverish.

'Go away,' she said and her tone was husky and imploring. 'Oh, go away—please, please!'

After the kiss Henry Brownrigg was human again and no longer the fiend-possessed soul in torment he had been while waiting in the lane. Now he could behave normally, for a time at least.

'All right,' he said, and added so lightly that she was deceived, 'going out with Peter Hill again this afternoon?'

The girl's lips trembled and her eyes were pleading.

'I'm trying to get free,' she said. 'Don't you see I'm trying to get free from you? It's not easy.'

Henry Brownrigg stared at her inquisitively for a full minute. Then he laughed shortly and explosively and strode away back down the lane at a great pace.

Henry Brownrigg went home. He walked very fast, his round eyes introspective but his step light and purposeful. His thoughts were pleasant. So Phyllis was there when he wanted her, there for the taking when the obstacle was once removed. That had been his only doubt. Now he was certain of it. The practical part of his project alone remained.

Small, relatively unimportant things like the new story the mottled ledger would have to tell when the insurance money was in the bank and Millie's small income was realized and reinvested crowded into his mind, but he brushed them aside impatiently. This afternoon he must be grimly practical. There was delicate work to do.

When he reached home Millie had gone over to her mother's.

It was also early-closing day and young Perry was far away, bowling wides for the St. Anne's parish cricket club.

Mr Brownrigg went round the house carefully and made sure that all the doors were locked. The shop shutters were up too, and he knew from careful observation that they permitted no light from within to escape.

He removed his jacket and donned his working overall, switched on the lights, locked the door between the shop and the living-room, and set to work.

He knew exactly what he had to do. Millie had been taking five Fender's pills regularly now for eight days. Each pill contained 1/16 gram Nativelle's Digitalin, and the stuff was cumulative. No wonder she had been complaining of biliousness and headaches lately! Millie was a hopeless fool.

He took out the bottle of Tincture Digitalin, which had come when young Perry had given him such a scare, and looked at it. He wished he had risked it and bought the Quevenne's, or the freshly powdered leaves. He wouldn't have had all this trouble now.

Still, he hadn't taken the chance, and on second thoughts he was glad. As it was, the wholesalers couldn't possibly notice anything unusual in his order. There could be no inquiry: it meant he need never worry—afterwards.

He worked feverishly as his thoughts raced on. He knew the dose. All that had been worked out months before when the idea had first occurred to him, and he had gone over this part of the proceedings again and again in his mind so that there could be no mistake, no slip.

Nine drachms of the tincture had killed a patient with no digitalin already in the system. But then the tincture was notoriously liable to deteriorate. Still, this stuff was fresh; barely six days old if the wholesalers could be trusted. He had thought of that.

He prepared his burner and the evaporator. It took a long time. Although he was so practised, his hands were unsteady and clumsy, and the irritant fumes got into his eyes.

Suddenly he discovered that it was nearly four o'clock. He was panic-stricken. Only two hours and Millie would come back, and there was a lot to be done.

As the burner did its work his mind moved rapidly. Digitalin was so difficult to trace afterwards; that was the beauty of it. Even the great Tardieu had been unable to state positively if it was digitalin that had been used in the Pommeraise case, and that after the most exhaustive P.M. and tests on frogs and all that sort of thing.

Henry Brownrigg's face split into the semblance of a smile. Old Crupiner was no Tardieu. Crupiner would not advise a P.M. if he could possibly avoid it. He'd give the certificate all right; his mind was prepared for it. Probably he wouldn't even come and look at the body.

Millie's stupid, placid body. Henry Brownrigg put the thought from him. No use getting nervy now.

A shattering peal on the back door startled him so much that he nearly upset his paraphernalia. For a moment he stood breathing wildly, like a trapped animal, but he pulled himself together in the end, and, changing into his coat, went down to answer the summons.

He locked the shop door behind him, smoothed his hair, and opened the back door confident that he looked normal, even ordinary.

But the small boy with the evening paper did not wait for his Saturday's sixpence but rushed away after a single glance at Mr Brownrigg's face. He was a timid twelve-year-old, however, who often imagined things, and his employer, an older boy, cuffed him for the story and made a mental note to call for the money himself on the Monday night.

The effect of the incident on Henry Brownrigg was considerable. He went back to his work like a man in a nightmare, and for the rest of the proceedings he kept his mind resolutely on the physical task.

At last it was done.

He turned out the burner, scoured the evaporator, measured the toxic dose carefully, adding to it considerably to be on the safe side. After all, one could hardly overdo it; that was the charm of this stuff.

Then he effectively disposed of the residue and felt much better.

He had locked the door and changed his coat again before he noticed the awful thing. A layer of fine dust on the top of one of the bottles first attracted his attention. He removed it with fastidious care. He hated a frowsy shop.

He had replaced his handkerchief before he saw the showcase ledge and the first glimmering of the dreadful truth percolated his startled mind.

From the ledge his eyes travelled to the counter top, to the dummy cartoons, to the bottles and jars, to the window shutters, to the very floor.

Great drops appeared on Henry Brownrigg's forehead. There was not an inch of surface in the whole shop that was innocent of the thinnest, faintest coat of yellowish dust.

Digitalin! Digitalin over the whole shop! Digitalin over the whole world! The evidence of his guilt everywhere, damning, unescapable, clear to the first intelligent observer.

Henry Brownrigg stood very still.

Gradually his brain, cool at the bidding of the instinct of selfpreservation, began to work again. Delay. That was the all-important note. Millie must not take the capsule tonight as he had planned. Not tonight, nor tomorrow. Millie must not die until every trace of that yellow dust had been driven from the shop.

Swiftly he rearranged his plan. Tonight he must behave as usual and tomorrow, when Millie went to church, he must clear off the worst of the stuff before young Perry noticed anything.

Then on Monday he would make an excuse and have the vacuum cleaning people in. They came with a great machine and put pipes in through the window. He had often said he would have it done.

They worked quickly; so on Tuesday...

Meanwhile, normality. That was the main thing. He must do nothing to alarm Millie or excite her curiosity.

It did not occur to him that there would be a grim irony in getting Millie to help him dust the shop that evening. But he dismissed the idea. They'd never do it thoroughly in the time.

He washed in the kitchen and went back into the hall. A step on the stairs above him brought a scream to his throat which he only just succeeded in stifling.

It was Millie. She had come in the back way without him hearing her, heaven knew how long before.

'I've borrowed a portiere curtain from Mother for your bedroom door, Henry,' she said mildly. 'You won't be troubled by the draught up there any more. It's such a good thick one. I've just been fixing it up. It looks very nice.'

Henry Brownrigg made a noise which might have meant anything. His nerves had gone to pieces.

Her next remark was reassuring, however; so reassuring that he almost laughed aloud.

'Oh, Henry,' she said, 'you only gave me four of those pills today, dear. You won't forget the other one, will you?'

'Cold ham from the cooked meat shop, cold tinned peas, potato salad and Worcester sauce. What a cook! What a cook I've married, my dear Millie.'

Henry Brownrigg derived a vicious pleasure from the clumsy sarcasm, and when Millie's pale face became wooden he was gratified.

As he sat at the small table and looked at her he was aware of a curious phenomenon. The woman stood out from the rest of the room's contents as though she alone was in relief. He saw every line of her features, every fold of her dark cotton foulard dress, as though they were drawn with a thick black pencil.

Millie was silent. Even her usual flow of banality had dried up, and he was glad of it.

He found himself regarding her dispassionately, as though she had been a stranger. He did not hate her, he decided. On the contrary, he was prepared to believe that she was quite an estimable, practicable person in her own limited fashion. But she was in the way.

This plump, fatuous creature, not even different in her very obtuseness from many of the other matrons in the town, had committed the crowning impudence of getting in the way of Henry Brownrigg. She, this ridiculous, lowly woman, actually stood between Henry Brownrigg and the inmost desires of his heart.

It was an insight into the state of the Chemist's mind that at that moment nothing impressed him so forcibly as her remarkable audacity.

Monday, he thought. Monday, and possibly Tuesday, and then... Millie cleared away.

Mr Brownrigg drank his first glass of whisky and soda with a relish he did not often experience. For him the pleasure of his Saturday night libations lay in the odd sensation he experienced when really drunk.

When Henry Brownrigg was a sack of limp, uninviting humanity to his wife and the rest of the world, to himself he was a quiet, all-powerful ghost, seated, comfortable and protected, in the shell of his body, able to see and comprehend everything, but too mighty and too important to direct any of the drivelling little matters which made up his immediate world.

On these occasions Henry Brownrigg tasted godhead.

The evening began like all the others, and by the time there was but an inch of amber elixir in the square bottle, Millie and the dust in the shop and Doctor Crupiner had become in his mind as ants and ant burdens, while he towered above them, a colossus in mind and power.

When the final inch had dwindled to a yellow stain in the bottom of the white glass bottle. Mr Brownrigg sat very still. In a few minutes now he would attain the peak of that ascendancy over his fellow mortals when the body, so important to them, was for him literally nothing; not even a dull encumbrance, not even a nerveless covering but a nothingness, an unimportant, unnoticed element.

When Millie came in at last a pin could have been thrust deep into Mr Brownrigg's flesh and he would not have noticed it.

It was when he was in bed, his useless body clad in clean pyjamas, that he noticed that Millie was not behaving quite as usual. She had folded his clothes neatly on the chair at the end of the bed when he saw her peering at something intently.

He followed her eyes and saw for the first time the new portiere curtain. It certainly was a fine affair, a great, thick, heavy plush thing that looked as though it would stop any draught there ever had been.

He remembered clearly losing his temper with Millie in front of young Perry one day, and, searching in his mind for a suitable excuse, had invented this draught beneath his bedroom door. And there wasn't one, his ghost remembered; that was the beauty of it. The door fitted tightly in the jamb. But it gave Millie something to worry about.

Millie went out of the room without extinguishing the lights. He tried to call out to her and only then realized the disadvantage of being a disembodied spirit. He could not speak, of course.

He was lying puzzled at this obvious flaw in his omnipotence when he heard her go downstairs instead of crossing into her room. He was suddenly furious and would have risen, had it been possible. But in the midst of his anger he remembered something amusing and lay still, inwardly convulsed with secret laughter.

Soon Millie would be dead. Dead-dead-dead. Millie would be stupid no longer.

Millie would appal him by her awful mindlessness no more.

Millie would be dead.

She came up again and stepped softly into the room.

The alcohol was beginning to take its full effect now and he could not move his head. Soon oblivion would come and he would leave his body and rush off into the exciting darkness, not to return until the dawn.

He saw only Millie's head and shoulders when she came into his line of vision. He was annoyed. She still had those thick black lines round her, and there was an absorbed expression upon her face which he remembered seeing before when she was engrossed in some particularly difficult household task.

She switched out the light and then went over to the far window. He was interested now, and saw her pull up the blinds.

Then to his astonishment he heard the crackle of paper; not an ordinary crackle, but something familiar, something he had heard hundreds of times before.

He placed it suddenly. Sticky paper. His own reel of sticky paper from the shop.

He was so cross with her for touching it that for some moments he did not wonder what she was doing with it, and it was not until he saw her silhouetted against the second row of panes that he guessed. She was sticking up the window cracks.

His ghost laughed again. The draught. Silly, stupid Millie trying to stop the draught.

She pulled down the blinds and turned on the light again. Her face was mild and expressionless as ever, her blue eyes vacant and foolish.

He saw her go to the dressing-table, still moving briskly, as she always did when working about the house.

Once again the phenomenon he had noticed at the evening meal became startlingly apparent. He saw her hand and its contents positively glowing because of its black outline, thrown up in high relief against the white table cover.

Millie was putting two pieces of paper there: one white with a deckle edge, one blue and familiar.

Henry Brownrigg's ghost yammered in its prison. His body ceased to be negligible: it became a coffin, a sealed, leaden coffin suffocating him in its senseless shell. He fought to free himself, to stir that mighty weight, to move.

Millie knew.

The white paper with the deckle edge was a letter from Phyllis out of the drawer in the shop, and the blue paper—he remembered it now—the blue paper he had left in the dirty developing bath.

He re-read his own pencilled words as clearly as if his eye had become possessed of telescopic sight:

'Millie dear, this does explain itself, doesn't it?'

And then his name, signed with a flourish. He had been so pleased with himself when he had written it.

He fought wildly. The coffin was made of glass now, thick, heavy glass which would not respond to his greatest effort.

Millie was hesitating. She had picked up Phyllis's letter. Now she was reading it again.

He saw her frown and tear the paper into shreds, thrusting the pieces into the pocket of her cardigan.

Henry Brownrigg, understood. Millie was sorry for Phyllis. For all her obtuseness she had guessed at some of the girl's piteous infatuation and had decided to keep her out of it.

What then? Henry Brownrigg writhed inside his inanimate body.

Millie was back at the table now. She was putting something else there. What was it? Oh, what was it?

The ledger! He saw it plainly, the old, mottled ledger, whose story was plain for any fool coroner to read and misunderstand.

Millie had turned away now. He hardly noticed her pause before the fireplace. She did not stoop. Her felt-shod slipper flipped the gas tap over.

Then she passed out of the door, extinguishing the light as she went. He heard the rustle of the thick curtain as she drew the wood close. There was an infinitesimal pause and then the key turned in the lock.

She had behaved throughout the whole proceeding as though she had been getting dinner or tidying the spare room.

In his prison Henry Brownrigg's impotent ghost listened. There was a hissing from the far end of the room.

In the attic, although he could not possibly hear it, he knew the metre ticked every two or three seconds.

Henry Brownrigg saw in a vision the scene in the morning. Every room in the house had the same key, so Millie would have no difficulty in explaining that on awakening she had noticed the smell of gas and, on finding her husband's door locked, had opened it with her own key.

The ghost stirred in its shell. Once again the earth and earthly incidents looked small and negligible. The oblivion was coming, the darkness was waiting; only now it was no longer exciting darkness.

The shell moved. He felt it writhe and choke. It was fighting—fighting—fighting.

The darkness drew him. He was no longer conscious of the shell now. It had been beaten. It had given up the fight.

The streak of light beneath the blind where the street lamp shone was fading. Fading. Now it was gone.

As Henry Brownrigg's ghost crept out into the cold a whisper came to it, ghastly in its conviction:

'They never get caught, that kind. They're too dull, too practical, too unimaginative. They never get caught.'

HAUNTED VILLAGES

Lt. Col. W.H. Sleeman

On the 16th, we came on nine miles to Amabe, the frontier village of the Jansee territory, bordering upon Duteea, where I had to receive the farewell visits of many members of the Jansee parties, who came on to have a quiet opportunity to assure me, that whatever may be the final order of the supreme government, they will do their best for the good of the people and the state, in whose welfare I feel great interest, for I have always considered Jansee among the native states of Bundelcund as a kind of oasis in the desert—the only one in which man can accumulate property with the confidence of being permitted by its rulers freely to display and enjoy it. I had also to receive the visit of messengers from the Rajah of Duteea, at whose capital we were to encamp the next day; and finally, to take leave of my amiable little friend the Sureemunt, who here left me on his return to Saugor, with a heavy heart I really believe.

We talked of the common belief among the agricultural classes, of villages being haunted by the spirits of ancient proprietors, whom it was thought necessary to propitiate. 'He knew,' he said, 'many instances where these spirits were so very froward, that the present heads of the villages which they haunted, and the members of their little communities, found it almost impossible to keep them in good humour; and their cattle and children were, in consequence, always liable to serious accidents of one kind or another. Sometimes they were bitten by snakes, sometimes became possessed by devils; and at others, were thrown down and beaten most unmercifully.' Any person who falls down in an epileptic fit, is supposed to be thrown down by a ghost, or possessed by a devil. They feel little of our mysterious dread of ghosts—a sound drubbing is what they dread from them; and he who hurts himself in one of these fits is considered to have got it. 'As for himself, whenever he found any one of the villages upon his estate haunted by the spirit of an old Patel, (village proprietor,) he always made a point of giving him a neat little shrine; and having it well endowed and attended, to keep him in good humour: this he thought was a duty that every landlord owed to his tenants!' Ramchund, the pundit, said, 'That villages which had been held by old Gond (mountaineer) proprietors were more liable than any other to those kinds of visitations—that it was easy to say what village was and was not haunted; but often exceedingly difficult to discover to whom the ghost belonged! This once discovered, his nearest surviving relation was, of course, expected to take steps to put him to rest; but,' said he, 'it is wrong to suppose that the ghost of an old proprietor must be always doing mischief—he is often the best friend of the cultivators, and of the present proprietor, too, if he treats him with proper respect; for he will not allow the people of any other village to encroach upon their boundaries with impunity; and they will be saved all the expense and annoyance of a reference to the Adawlut (judicial tribunals) for the settlement of boundary disputes. It will not cost much to conciliate these spirits; and the money is generally well laid out!'

Several anecdotes were told me in illustration; and all that I could urge against the probability or possibility of such visitations appeared to them very inconclusive and unsatisfactory; they mentioned the case of the family of village proprietors in the

Saugor district, who had for several generations, at every new settlement, insisted upon having the name of the spirit of the old proprietor of another tribe inserted in the lease instead of their own, and thereby secured his good graces on all occasions. Mr Fraser had before mentioned this case to me. In August 1834, while engaged in the settlement of the land revenue of the Saugor district for twenty years, he was about to deliver the lease of the estate made out in due form to the head of the family, a very honest and respectable old gentleman, when he asked him, respectfully, in whose name it had been made out? 'In yours to be sure; have you renewed your lease for twenty years?' The old man, in a state of great alarm, begged him to have it altered immediately, or he and his family would all be destroyed—that the spirit of the ancient proprietor presided over the village community and its interests; and that all affairs of importance were transacted in his name. 'He is,' said the old man, 'a very jealous spirit; and will not admit of any living man being considered, for a moment, as a proprietor or joint proprietor of the estate! It has been held by me and my ancestors immediately under government for many generations; but the lease deeds have always been made out in his name; and ours have been inserted merely as his managers, or bailiffs—were this good old rule, under which we have so long prospered, to be now infringed, we should all perish under his anger.' Mr Fraser found, upon inquiry, that this had really been the case; and, to relieve the old man and his family from their fears, he had the papers made out afresh, and the *ghost* inserted as the proprietor! The modes of flattering and propitiating these beings, natural and supernatural, who are supposed to have the power to do mischief, are endless.

While I was in charge of the district of Nursingpore, in the valley of the Nerbudda, in 1823, a cultivator of the village of Bedoo, about twelve miles distant from my court, was one day engaged in the cultivation of his field on the border of the village of Burkhara, which was supposed to be haunted by the spirit of an old proprietor, whose temper was so froward and violent that the lands could hardly be let for anything; for hardly any man would venture to cultivate them lest he might unintentionally incur his ghostship's displeasure. The poor cultivator, after begging his pardon in secret, ventured to drive his plough a few yards beyond the proper line of his boundary, and thus to add half an acre of the lands of Burkhara to his own little tenement, which was situated in Bedoo. That very night his only son was bitten by a snake, and his two bullocks were seized with the murrain. In terror he went off to the village temple, confessed his sin, and vowed not only to restore the half acre of land to the village of Burkhara, but to build a very handsome shrine upon the spot as a perpetual sign of his repentance. The boy and the bullocks all three recovered, and the shrine was built; and is, I believe, still to be seen as the boundary mark!

The fact was, that the village stood upon and elevated piece of ground rising out of a moist plain, and a colony of snakes had taken up their abode in it. The bites of these snakes had, on many occasions, proved fatal; and such accidents were all attributed to the anger of a spirit, which was supposed to haunt the village. At one time, under the former government, no one would take a lease of the village on any terms; and it had become almost entirely deserted, though the soil was the finest in the whole district. With a view to remove the whole prejudices of the people, the governor, Goroba Pundit, took the lease himself at the rent of one thousand rupees a year; and in the month of June went from his residence, twelve miles, with ten of his own ploughs, to superintend the commencement of so perilous an undertaking. On reaching the middle of the village, situated on the top of the little hill, he alighted from his horse, sat down upon a carpet that had been spread for him under a large and beautiful banyan tree, and began to refresh himself with a pipe before going to work in the fields. As he quaffed his hookah, and railed at the follies of men, 'whose absurd superstitions had made them desert so beautiful a village with so noble a tree in its centre,' his eyes fell upon an enormous black snake which had coiled round one of its branches immediately over his head, and seemed as if resolved at once to pounce down and punish him for his blasphemy! He gave his pipe to his attendant, mounted his horse, from which the saddle had not yet been taken, and never pulled rein till he got home. Nothing could ever induce him to visit this village again, though he was afterwards employed under me as a native collector; and he has often told me, that he verily believed this was the spirit of the old landlord that he had unhappily neglected to propitiate before taking possession!

My predecessor in the civil charge of that district, the late Mr Lindsay, of the Bengal civil service, again tried to remove the prejudices of the people against the occupation and cultivation of this fine village. It had never been measured; and all the revenue officers, backed by all the farmers and cultivators of the neighbourhood, declared that the spirit of the old proprietor would never allow it to be so. Mr Lindsay was a good geometrician, and had long been in the habit of superintending his revenue surveys himself; and on this occasion he thought himself particularly called upon to do so. A new measuring cord was made for the occasion, and with fear and trembling all his officers attended him to the first field; but in measuring it the rope, by some accident, broke! Poor Lindsay was that morning taken ill, and obliged to return to Nursingpore, where he died soon after from fever. No man was ever more beloved by all classes of the people of his district than he was; and I believe there was not one person among them who did not believe him to have fallen a victim to the resentment of the spirit of the old proprietor. When I went to the village some years afterwards, the people in the neighbourhood all declared to me, that they saw the cord with which he was measuring, fly into a thousand pieces the moment the men attempted to straighten it over the first field.

A very respectable old gentleman from the Concan, or Malabar coast, told me one day, that every man there protects his field of corn and his fruit tree by dedicating it to one or other of the spirits which there abound, or confiding it to his guardianship. He sticks up something in the field, or ties on something to the tree, in the name of the said spirit, who from that moment feels himself responsible for its safe-keeping. If anyone, without permission from the proprietor, presumes to take either an ear of corn from the field, or fruit from the tree, he is sure to be killed outright or made extremely ill. 'No other protection is required,' said the old gentleman, 'for our fields and fruit trees in that direction, though whole armies should have to march through them, I once saw a man come to the proprietor of a jack tree, embrace his feet, and in the most piteous manner implore his protection. He asked what was the matter. 'I took,' said the man, 'a jack from your tree yonder three days ago, as I passed at night; and I have been suffering dreadful agony in my stomach ever since. The spirit of the tree is upon me, and you only can pacify him.' The proprietor took up a bit of cow dung, moistened it, and made a mark with it upon the man's forehead in the *name of the spirit*, and put some of it into the knot of hair on the top of his head. He had no sooner done this, than the man's pains all left him, and he went off, vowing never again to give similar cause of offence to one of these guardian spirits.'

'Men,' said my old friend, 'do not die there in the same regulated spirit, with their thoughts directed exclusively towards God, as in other parts; and whether a man's spirit is to haunt the world or not after his death all depends on that.'

THE SQUAW

Bram Stoker

Nurnberg at the time was not so much exploited as it has been since then. Irving had not been playing *Faust*, and the very name of the old town was hardly known to the great bulk of the travelling public. My wife and I being in the second week of our honeymoon naturally wanted someone else to join our party, so that when the cheery stranger, Elias P. Hutcheson, hailing from Isthmian City, Bleeding Gulch, Maple Tree County, Neb., turned up at the station at Frankfort, and casually remarked that he was going on to see the most all-fired old Methusaleh of a town in Yurrup, and that he guessed that so much travelling alone was enough to send an intelligent, active citizen into the melancholy ward of a daft house, we took the pretty broad hint and suggested that we should join forces. We found, on comparing notes afterwards, that we had each intended to speak with some diffidence or hesitation so as not to appear too eager, such not being a good compliment to the success of our married life; but the effect was entirely marred by both of us beginning to speak at the same instant—stopping simultaneously and then going on together again. Anyhow, no matter how, it was done; and Elias P. Hutcheson became one of our party. Straightaway Amelia and I found the pleasant benefit; instead of quarrelling, as we had been doing, we found that the restraining influence of a third party was such that we now took every opportunity of spooning in odd corners. Amelia declares that ever since she has, as a result of that experience, advised all her friends to take a friend on the honeymoon. Well, we 'did' Nurnberg together, and much enjoyed the racy remarks of our Transatlantic friend, who, from his quaint speech and his wonderful stock of adventures, might have stepped out of a novel. We kept for the last object of interest in the city to be visited, the Burg, and on the day appointed for the visit strolled round the outer wall of the city by the eastern side.

The Burg is seated on a rock dominating the town, and an immensely deep fosse guards it on the northern side. Nurnberg has been happy in that it was never sacked; had it been it would certainly not be so spick and span perfect as it is at present. The ditch has not been used for centuries, and now its base is spread with tea—gardens and orchards, of which some of the trees are of quite respectable growth. As we wandered round the wall, dawdling in the hot July sunshine, we often paused to admire the views spread before us, and in especial the great plain covered with towns and villages and bounded with a blue line of hills, like a landscape of Claude Lorraine. From this we always turned with new delight to the city itself, with its myriad of quaint old gables and acre-wide red roofs dotted with dormer windows, tier upon tier. A little to our right rose the towers of the Burg, and nearer still, standing grim, the Torture Tower, which was, and is, perhaps, the most interesting place in the city. For centuries the tradition of the Iron Virgin of Nurnberg has been handed down as an instance of the horrors of cruelty of which man is capable; we had long looked forward to seeing it; and here at last was its home.

In one of our pauses we leaned over the wall of the moat and looked down. The garden seemed quite fifty or sixty feet below us, and the sun pouring into it with an intense, moveless heat like that of an oven. Beyond rose the grey, grim wall seemingly of endless height, and losing itself right and left in the angles of bastion and counterscarp. Trees and bushes crowned the wall, and above again towered the lofty houses on whose massive beauty Time has only set the hand of approval. The sun was hot and we were lazy; time was our own, and we lingered, leaning on the wall. Just below us was a pretty sight—a great black cat lying stretched in the sun, whilst round her gambolled prettily a tiny black kitten. The mother would wave her tail for the kitten to play with, or would raise her feet and push away the little one as an encouragement to further play. They were just at the foot of the wall, and Elias P. Hutcheson, in order to help the play, stooped and took from the walk a moderate-sized pebble.

'See!' he said, 'I will drop it near the kitten, and they will both wonder where it came from.'

'Oh, be careful,' said my wife; 'you might hit the dear little thing!'

'Not me, ma'am,' said Elias P. 'Why, I'm as tender as a Maine cherry tree. Lor, bless ye, I wouldn't hurt the poor pooty little critter more'n I'd scalp a baby. An' you may bet your variegated socks on that! See, I'll drop it fur away on the outside so's not to go near her!' Thus saying, he leaned over and held his arm out at full length and dropped the stone. It may be that there is some attractive force which draws lesser matters to greater; or more probably that the wall was not plumb but sloped to its base—we not noticing the inclination from above; but the stone fell with a sickening thud that came up to us through the hot air, right on the kitten's head, and shattered out its little brains then and there. The black cat cast a swift upward glance, and we saw her eyes like green fire fixed an instant on Elias P. Hutcheson; and then her attention was given to the kitten, which lay still with just a quiver other tiny limbs, whilst a thin red stream trickled from a gaping wound. With a muffled cry, such as a human being might give, she bent over the kitten licking its wound and moaning. Suddenly she seemed to realize that it was dead, and again threw her eyes up at us. I shall never forget the sight, for she looked the perfect incarnation of hate. Her green eyes blazed with lurid fire, and the white, sharp teeth seemed to almost shine through the blood which dabbled her mouth and whiskers. She gnashed her teeth, and her claws stood out stark and at full length on every paw. Then she made a wild rush up the wall as if to reach us, but when the momentum ended fell back and further added to her horrible appearance, for she fell on the kitten and rose with her black fur smeared with its brains and blood. Amelia turned quite faint, and I had to lift her back from the wall. There was a seat close by in shade of a spreading plane tree, and here I placed her whilst she composed herself Then I went back to Hutcheson, who stood without moving, looking down on the angry cat below.

As I joined him, he said:

'Wall, I guess that air the savagest beast I ever see—'cept once when an Apache squaw had an edge on a half-breed what they nicknamed "Splinters" 'cos of the way he fixed up heripapoose which he stole on a raid just to show that he appreciated the way they had given his mother the fire torture. She got that kinder look so set on her face that it jest seemed to grow there. She followed Splinters more'n three year till at last the braves got him and handed him over to her. They did say that no man, white or Injun, had ever been so long a-dying under the tortures of the Apaches. The only time I ever see her smile was when I wiped her out. I kem on the camp just in time to see Splinters pass in his checks, and he wasn't sorry to go either. He was a hard citizen, and though I never could shake with him after that papoose business'—for it was bitter bad, and he should have been a white man, for he looked like one—I see he had got paid out in full. Durn me, but I took a piece of his hide from one of his skinnin' posts an' had it made into a pocket-book. It's here now!' and he slapped the breast pocket of his coast.

Whilst he was speaking, the cat was continuing her frantic efforts to get up the wall. She would take a run back and then charge up, sometimes reaching an incredible height. She did not seem to mind the heavy fall which she got each time but started with renewed vigour; and at every tumble her appearance became more horrible. Hutcheson was a kind-hearted man—my wife and I had both noticed little acts of kindness to animals as well as to persons—and he seemed concerned at the state of fury to which the cat had wrought herself.

'Wall, now!' he said, 'I du declare that that poor critter seems quite desperate. There! there! poor thing, it was all an accident—though that won't bring back your little one to you. Say! I wouldn't have had such a thing happen for a thousand! Just shows what a clumsy fool of a man can do when he tries to play! Seems I'm too darned slipper-handed to even play with a cat. Say, Colonell'—it was a pleasant way he had to bestow titles freely—'I hope your wife don't hold no grudge against me on account of this unpleasantness. Why, I wouldn't have had it occur on no account.'

He came over to Amelia and apologized profusely, and she with her usual kindness of heart hastened to assure him that she quite understood that it was an accident. Then we all went again to the wall and looked over.

The cat missing Hutcheson's face had drawn back across the moat, and was sitting on her haunches as though ready to spring. Indeed, the very instant she saw him she did spring, and with a blind, unreasoning fury, which would have been grotesque, only that it was so frightfully real. She did not try to run up the wall, but simply launched herself at him as though hate and fury could lend her wings to pass straight through the great distance between them. Amelia, womanlike, got quite concerned and said to Elias P. in a warning voice:

'Oh! you must be very careful. That animal would try to kill you if she were here; her eyes look like positive murder.'

He laughed out jovially. 'Excuse me, ma'am,' he said, 'but I "can't help laughin'. Fancy a man that has fought grizzlies an' Injuns bein' careful of bein' murdered by a cat!'

When the cat heard him laugh, her whole demeanour seemed to change. She no longer tried to jump or run up the wall, but went quietly over, and sitting again beside the dead kitten, began to lick and fondle it as though it were alive.

'See!' said I, 'the effect of a really strong man. Even that animal in the midst other fury recognises the voice of a master, and bows to him!'

'Like a squaw!' was the only comment of Elias P. Hutcheson, as we moved on our way round the city fosse. Every now and then we looked over the wall and each time saw the cat following us. At first she had kept going back to the dead kitten, and then as the distance grew greater, she took it in her mouth and so followed. After a while, however, she abandoned this, for we saw her following all alone; she had evidently hidden the body somewhere. Amelia's alarm grew at the cat's persistence, and more than once she repeated her warning; but the American always laughed with amusement, till finally, seeing that she was beginning to be worried, he said:

'I say, ma'am, you needn't be skcered over that cat. I go heeled, I du!' Here he slapped his pistol pocket at the back of his lumbar region. 'Why, sooner'n have you worried, I'll shoot the critter, right here, an' risk the police interferin' with a citizen of the United States for carryin' arms contrairy to regulations!' As he spoke he looked over the wall, but the cat, on seeing him, retreated with a growl into a bed of tall flowers and was hidden. He went on: 'Blest if that ar critter ain't got more sense of what's good for her than most Christians. I guess we've seen the last of her! You bet, she'll go back now to that busted kitten and have a private funeral of it, all to herself!'

Amelia did not like to say more, lest he might, in mistaken kindness to her, fulfil his threat of shooting the cat: and so we went on and crossed the little wooden bridge leading to the gateway whence ran the steep paved roadway between the Burg and the pentagonal Torture Tower. As we crossed the bridge we saw the cat again down below us. When she saw us, her fury seemed to return and she made frantic efforts to get up the steep wall. Hutcheson laughed as he looked down at her, and said:

'Goodbye, old girl. Sorry I in-jured your feelin's, but you'll get over it in time! So long!' And then we passed through the long, dim archway and came to the gate of the Burg.

When we came out again after our survey of this most beautiful old place which not even the well-intentioned efforts of the Gothic restorers of forty years ago have been able to spoil—though their restoration was then glaring white—we seemed to have quite forgotten the unpleasant episode of the morning. The old lime tree with its great trunk gnarled with the passing of nearly nine centuries, the deep well cut through the heart of the rock by those captives of old, and the lovely view from the city wall whence we heard, spread over almost a full quarter of an hour, the multitudinous chimes of the city, had all helped to wipe out from our minds the incident of the slain kitten.

We were the only visitors who had entered the Torture Tower that morning—so at least said the old custodian—and as we had the place all to ourselves were able to make a minute and more satisfactory survey than would have otherwise been possible. The custodian, looking to us as the sole source of his gains for the day, was willing to meet our wishes in any way. The Torture Tower is truly a grim place, even now when many thousands of visitors have sent a stream of life, and the joy that follows life, into the place; but at the time I mention, it wore its grimmest and most gruesome aspect. The dust of ages seemed to have settled on it, and the darkness and the horror of its memories seem to have become sentient in a way that would have satisfied the Pantheistic souls of Philo or Spinoza. The lower chamber, where we entered, was seemingly, in its normal state, filled with incarnate darkness; even the hot sunlight streaming in through the door seemed to be lost in the vast thickness of the walls, and only showed the masonry rough as when the builder's scaffolding had come down, but coated with dust and marked here and there with patches of dark stain which, if walls could speak, could have given their own dread memories of fear and pain. We were glad to pass up the dusty wooden staircase, the custodian leaving the outer door open to light us somewhat on our way; for to our eyes the one long-wick'd, evil-smelling candle stuck in a sconce on the wall gave an inadequate light. When we came up through the open trap in the corner of the chamber overhead, Amelia held on to me so tightly that I could actually feel her heart beat. I must say for my own part that I was not surprised at her fear, for this room was even more gruesome than that below. Here there was certainly more light, but only just sufficient to realise the horrible surroundings of the place. The builders of the tower had evidently intended that only they who should gain the top should have any of the joys of light and prospect. There, as we had noticed from below, were ranges of windows, albeit of medieval smallness, but elsewhere in the tower were only a very few narrow slits such as were habitual in places of medieval defence. A few of these only lit the chamber, and these were so high up in the wall that from no part could the sky be seen through the thickness of the walls. In racks, and leaning in disorder against the walls, were a number of headsmen's swords, great double-handed weapons with broad blade and keen edge. Hard by were several blocks whereon the necks of the victims had lain, with here and there deep notches where the steel had bitten through the guard of flesh and shored into the wood. Round the chamber, placed in all sorts of irregular ways, were many implements of torture which made one's heart ache to see—chairs full of spikes which gave instant and excruciating pain; chairs and couches with dull knobs whose torture was seemingly less, but which, though slower, were equally efficacious; racks, belts, boots, gloves, collars, all made for compressing at will; steel baskets in which the head could be slowly crushed into a pulp if necessary; watchmen's hooks with long handle and knife that cut at resistance—this a specialty of the old Nurnberg police system; and many, many other devices for man's injury to man. Amelia grew quite pale with the horror of things, but fortunately did not faint, for being a little overcome she sat down on a torture chair, but jumped up again with a shriek, all tendency to faint gone. We both pretended that it was the injury done to her dress by the dust of the chair and the rusty spikes which had upset her, and Mr Hutcheson acquiesced in accepting the explanation with a kind-hearted laugh.

But the central object in the whole of this chamber of horrors was the engine known as the Iron Virgin, which stood near the centre of the room. It was a rudely-shaped figure of a woman, something of the bell order, or, to make a closer comparison, of the figure of Mrs Noah in the children's Ark, but without that slimness of waist and perfect *rondeur* of hip which marks the aesthetic type of the Noah family One would hardly have recognized it as intended for a human figure at all had not the founder shaped on the forehead a rude semblance of a woman's face. This machine was coated with rust without, and covered with dust; a rope was fastened to a ring in the front of the figure, about where the waist should have been, and was drawn through a pulley, fastened on the wooden pillar which sustained the flooring above. The custodian pulling this rope showed that a section of the front was hinged like a door at one side; we then saw that the engine was of considerable thickness, leaving just room enough inside for a man to be placed. The door was of equal thickness and of great weight, for it took the custodian all his strength, aided though he was by the contrivance of the pulley, to open it. This weight was partly due to the fact that the door was of manifest purpose hung so as to throw its weight downwards, so that it might shut of its own accord when the strain was released. The inside was honeycombed with rust—nay more, the rust alone that comes through time would hardly have eaten so deep into the iron walls; the rust of the cruel stains was deep indeed! It was only, however, when we came to look at the inside of the door that the diabolical intention was manifest to the full. Here were several long spikes, square and massive, broad at the base and sharp at the points, placed in such a position that when the door should close, the upper ones would pierce the eyes of the victim and the lower ones his heart and vitals. The sight was too much for poor Amelia, and this time she fainted dead off, and I had to carry her down the stairs and place her on a bench outside till she recovered. That she felt it to the quick was afterwards shown by the fact that my eldest son bears to this day a rude birthmark on his breast, which has, by family consent, been accepted as representing the Nurnberg Virgin.

When we got back to the chamber, we found Hutcheson still opposite the Iron Virgin; he had been evidently philosophizing, and now gave us the benefits of this thought in the shape of a sort of exordium.

'Wall, I guess I've been learnin' somethin' here while madam has been getting over her faint. 'Pears to me that we're a long way behind the times on our side of the big drink. We uster think out on the plains that the Injun could give us points in tryin' to make a man on comfortable; but I guess your old medieval law-and-order party could raise him every time. Splinters was pretty good in his bluff on the squaw, but this here young miss held a straight flush all high on him. The points of them spikes air sharp enough still, though even the edges air eaten out by what uster be on them. It'd be a god thing for our Indian section to get some specimens of this here play-toy to send round to the Reservations jest to knock the stuffin' out of the bucks, and the squaws too, by showing them as how old civilization lays over them at their best. Guess but I'll get in that box a minute jest to see how it feels!'

'Oh no! no!!' said Amelia. 'It is too terrible!'

'Guess, ma'am, nothin's too terrible to the explorin' mind. I've been in some queer places in my time. Spent a night inside a dead horse while a prairie fire swept over me in Montana Territory—an' another time slept inside a dead buffler when the Comanches was on the war path an' didn't keer to leave my kyard on them. I've been two days in a caved-in tunnel in the Billy Broncho gold mine in New Mexico an' was one of the four shut up for three parts of a day in the caisson what slid over on her side when we was settin' the foundations of the Buffalo Bridge. I've not funked an odd experience yet, an'

I don't propose to begin now!'

We saw that he was set on the experiment, so I said: 'Well, hurry up, old man, and get through it quick!'

'All right, General,' said he, 'but I calculate we ain't quite ready yet. The gentlemen, my predecessors, what stood in that thar canister, didn't volunteer for the office—not much! And I guess there was some ornamental tyin' up before the big stroke was made. I want to go into this thing fair and square, so I must get fixed up proper first. I dare say this old galoot can rise some string and tie me up accordin' to sample?'

This was said interrogatively to the old custodian, but the latter, who understood the drift of his speech, though perhaps not appreciating to the full the niceties of dialect and imagery, shook his head. His protest was, however, only formal and made to be overcome. The American thrust a gold piece into his hand, saying, 'Take it, pard! it's your pot; and don't be skcer'd. This ain't no necktie party that you're asked to assist in!' He produced some thin frayed rope and proceeded to bind our companion with sufficient strictness for the purpose. When the upper part of his body was bound, Hutcheson said:

'Hold on a moment, Judge. Guess I'm too heavy for you to tote into the canister. You jest let me walk in, and then you can wash up regardin' my legs!'

Whilst speaking he had backed himself into the opening which was just enough to hold him. It was a close fit and no mistake. Amelia looked on with fear in her eyes, but she evidently did not like to say anything. Then the custodian completed his task by tying the American's feet together so that he was now absolutely helpless and fixed in his voluntary prison. He seemed to really enjoy it, and the incipient smile which was habitual to his face blossomed into actuality as he said:

'Guess this here Eve was made out of the rib of a dwarf!

There ain't much room for a full-grown citizen of the United States to hustle. We uster make our coffins more roomier in Idaho territory. Now, Judge, you jest begin to let this door down, slow, on to me. I want to feel the same pleasure as the other jays had when those spikes began to move toward their eyes!'

'Oh no! no! no!' broke in Amelia hysterically. 'It is too terrible! I can't bear to see it!—I can't I can't!'

But the American was obdurate. 'Say, Colonel,' said he, 'why not take Madame for a little promenade? I wouldn't hurt her feelin's for the world; but now that I am here, havin' kem eight thousand miles, wouldn't it be too hard to give up the very experience I've been pinin' an' pantin' fur? A man can't get to feel like canned goods every time! Me and the Judge here'll fix up this thing in no time, an' then you'll come back, an' we'll all laugh together!'

Once more the resolution that is born of curiosity triumphed, and Amelia stayed holding tight to my arm and shivering whilst the custodian began to slacken slowly inch by inch the rope that held back the iron door. Hutcheson's face was positively radiant as his eyes followed the first movement of the spikes.

'Wall!' he said, 'I guess I've not had enjoyment like this since I left Noo York. Bar a scrap with a French sailor at Wapping—an' that warn't much of a picnic neither—I've not had a show fur real pleasure in this dod-rotted Continent, where there ain't no b'ars nor no Injuns, an' wheer nary man goes heeled. Slow there, Judge! Don't you rush this business! I want a show for my money this game—I du!'

The custodian must have had in him some of the blood of his predecessors in that ghastly tower, for he worked the engine with a deliberate and excruciating slowness which after five minutes, in which the outer edge of the door had not moved half as many inches, began to overcome Amelia. I saw her lips whiten, and felt her hold upon my arm relax. I looked around an instant for a place whereon to lay her, and when I looked at her again found that her eye had become fixed on the side of the Virgin. Following its direction I saw the black cat crouching out of sight. Her green eyes shone like danger lamps in the gloom of the place, and their colour was heightened by the blood which still smeared her coat and reddened her mouth. I cried out:

'The cat! look out for the cat!' for even then she sprang out before the engine. At this moment she looked like a triumphant demon. Her eyes blazed with ferocity, her hair bristled out till she seemed twice her normal size, and her tail lashed about as does a tiger's when the quarry is before it. Elias P. Hutcheson when he saw her was amused, and his eyes positively sparkled with fun as he said:

'Darned if the squaw hain't got on all her war paint! Jest give her a shove off if she comes any of her tricks on me, for I'm so fixed everlastingly by the boss, that durn my skin if I can keep my eyes from her if she wants them! Easy there, Judge! don't you slack that ar rope or I'm euchered!'

At this moment Amelia completed her faint, and I had to clutch hold of her round the waist or she would have fallen to the floor. Whilst attending to her I saw the black cat crouching for a spring, and jumped up to turn the creature out.

But at that instant, with a sort of hellish scream, she hurled herself, not as we expected at Hutcheson, but straight at the face of the custodian. Her claws seemed to be tearing wildly as one sees in the Chinese drawings of the dragon rampant, and as I looked

I saw one of them light on the poor man's eye and actually tear through it and down his cheek, leaving a wide band of red where the blood seemed to spurt from every vein.

With a yell of sheer terror which came quicker than even his sense of pain, the man leaped back, dropping as he did so the rope which held back the iron door. I jumped for it, but was too late, for the cord ran like lightning through the pulley-block, and the heavy mass fell forward from its own weight.

As the door closed I caught a glimpse of our poor companion's face. He seemed frozen with terror. His eyes stared with a horrible anguish, as if dazed, and no sound came from his lips.

And then the spikes did their work. Happily the end was quick, for when I wrenched open the door they had pierced so deep that they had locked in the bones of the skull through which they had crushed, and actually tore him—it—out of his iron prison till, bound as he was, he fell at full length with a sickly thud upon the floor, the face turning upward as he fell.

I rushed to my wife, lifted her up and carried her out, for I feared For her very reason if she should wake from her faint to such a scene. I laid her on the bench outside and ran back. Leaning against the wooden column was the custodian moaning in pain whilst he held his reddening handkerchief to his eyes. And sitting on the head of the poor American was the cat, purring loudly as she licked the blood which trickled through the gashed socket of his eyes.

I think no one will call me cruel because I seized one of the old executioner's swords and shore her in two as she sat.

THE DUEL

Wilkie Collins

The doctors could do no more for the dowager Lady Berrick. When the medical advisers of a lady who has reached seventy years of age recommend the mild climate of the South of France, they mean in plain language that they have arrived at the end of their resources. Her ladyship gave the mild climate a fair trial, and then decided (as she herself expressed it) to 'die at home'. Travelling slowly, she had reached Paris at the date when I last heard of her. It was then the beginning of November. A week later, I met with her nephew, Lewis Romayne, at the club.

'What brings you to London at this time of the year?' I asked.

'The fatality that pursues me,' he answered grimly. 'I am one of the unluckiest men living.'

He was thirty years old; he was not married; he was the enviable possessor of the tiny old country seat, called Vange Abbey; he had no poor relations; and he was one of the handsomest men in England. When I add that I am, myself, a retired army officer, with a wretched income, a disagreeable wife, four ugly children, and a burden of fifty years on my back, no one will be surprised to hear that I answered Romayne, with bitter sincerity, in these words:

'I wish to Heaven I could change places with you!'

'I wish to Heaven you could!' he burst out, with equal sincerity on his side. 'Read that.'

He handed me a letter addressed to him by the travelling

medical attendant of Lady Berrick. After resting in Paris, the patient had continued her homeward journey as far as Boulogne. In her suffering condition, she was liable to sudden fits of caprice. An insurmountable horror of the Channel passage had got possession of her: she positively refused to be taken on board the steamboat. In this difficulty, the lady who held the post of her 'companion' had ventured on a suggestion. Would Lady Berrick consent to make the Channel passage if her nephew came to Boulogne expressly to accompany her on the voyage? The reply had been so immediately favourable, that the doctor lost no time in communicating with Mr Lewis Romayne. This was the substance of the letter.

It was needless to ask any more questions—Romayne was plainly on his way to Boulogne. I gave him some useful information. 'Try the oysters,' I said, 'at the restaurant on the pier.'

He never even thanked me. He was thinking entirely of himself.

'Just look at my position,' he said. 'I detest Boulogne; I cordially share my aunt's horror of the Channel passage; I had looked forward to some months of happy retirement in the country among my books—and what happens to me? I am brought to London in this season of fogs, to travel by the tidal train at seven tomorrow morning—and all for a woman with whom I have no sympathies in common. If I am not an unlucky man—who is?'

He spoke in a tone of vehement irritation which seemed to me, under the circumstances, to be simply absurd. But *my* nervous system is not the irritable system—sorely tried by night study and strong tea—of my friend Romayne. 'It's only a matter of two days,' I remarked, by way of reconciling him to his situation.

'How do I know that?' he retorted. 'In two days the weather may be stormy. In two days she may be too ill to be moved. Unfortunately, I am her heir; and I am told I must submit to any whim that seizes her. I'm rich enough already; I don't want her money. Besides, I dislike all travelling—and especially travelling alone. You are an idle man. If you were a good friend, you would offer to go with me.' He added, with the delicacy which was one of the redeeming points in his wayward character, 'Of course as my guest.'

I had known him long enough not to take offence at his reminding me, in this considerate way, that I was a poor man. The proposed change of scene tempted me. What did I care for the Channel passage? Besides, there was the irresistible attraction of getting away from home.

The end of it was that I accepted Romayne's invitation.

II

Shortly after noon, on the next day, we were established at Boulogne—near Lady Berrick, but not at her hotel. 'If we live in the same house,' Romayne reminded me, 'we shall be bored by the companion and the doctor. Meetings on the stairs, you know, and exchanging bows and small talk.' He hated those trivial conventionalities of society, in which other people delight. When somebody once asked him in what company he felt most at ease? He made a shocking answer—he said, 'In the company of dogs.'

I waited for him on the pier while he went to see her ladyship. He joined me again with his bitterest smile. 'What did I tell you? She is not well enough to see me today. The doctor looks grave, and the companion puts her handkerchief to her eyes. We may be kept in this place for weeks to come.'

The afternoon proved to be rainy. Our early dinner was a

bad one. This last circumstance tried his temper sorely. He was no gourmand; the question of cookery was (with him) purely a matter of digestion. Those late hours of study and that abuse of tea to which I have already alluded, had sadly injured his stomach. The doctors warned him of serious consequences to his nervous system, unless he altered his habits. He had little faith in medical science, and he greatly overrated the restorative capacity of his constitution. So far as I know, he had always neglected the doctors' advice.

The weather cleared towards evening, and we went out for a walk. We passed a church—a Roman Catholic church, of course—the doors of which were still open. Some poor women were kneeling at their prayers in the dim light. 'Wait a minute,' said Romayne. 'I am in a vile temper. Let me try to put myself into a better frame of mind.'

I followed him into the church. He knelt down in a dark corner by himself. I confess I was surprised. He had been baptized in the Church of England; but, so far as outward practice was concerned, he belonged to no religious community. I had often heard him speak with sincere reverence and admiration of the spirit of Christianity—but he never, to my knowledge, attended any place of public worship. When we met again outside the church, I asked if he had been converted to the Roman Catholic faith.

'No,' he said. 'I hate the inveterate striving of that priesthood after social influence and political power as cordially as the fiercest Protestant living. But let us not forget that the Church of Rome has great merits to set against great faults. Its system is administered with an admirable knowledge of the higher needs of human nature. Take as one example what you have just seen. The solemn tranquillity of that church, the poor people praying near me, the few words of prayer by which I silently united myself to my fellow creatures have calmed me, and done me good. In our country I should have found the church closed, out-of-service hours.' He took my arm, and abruptly changed the subject. 'How will you occupy yourself,' he asked, 'if my aunt receives me tomorrow?'

I assured him that I should easily find ways and means of getting through the time. The next morning a message came from Lady Berrick, to say that she would see her nephew after breakfast. Left by myself, I walked towards the pier, and met with a man who asked me to hire his boat. He had lines and bait, at my service. Most unfortunately, as the event proved, I decided on occupying an hour or two by sea fishing.

The wind shifted while we were out, and before we could get back to the harbour, the tide had turned against us. It was six o'clock when I arrived at the hotel. A little open carriage was waiting at the door. I found Romayne impatiently expecting me, and no signs of dinner on the table. He informed me that he had accepted an invitation, in which I was included, and promised to explain everything in the carriage.

Our driver took the road that led towards the High Town. I subordinated my curiosity to my sense of politeness, and asked for news of his aunt's health.

'She is seriously ill, poor soul,' he said. 'I am sorry I spoke so petulantly and so unfairly when we met at the club. The near prospect of death has developed qualities in her nature which I ought to have seen before this. No matter how it may be delayed, I will patiently wait her time for the crossing to England.'

So long as he believed himself to be in the right, he was, as to his actions and opinions, one of the most obstinate men I ever met with. But once let him be convinced that he was wrong, and he rushed into the other extreme—became needlessly distrustful of himself, and needlessly eager in seizing his opportunity of making atonement. In this latter mood he was capable (with the best intentions) of committing acts of the most childish imprudence. With some misgivings, I asked how he had amused himself in my absence.

'I waited for you,' he said, 'till I lost all patience, and went out for a walk. First, I thought of going to the beach, but the smell of the harbour drove me back into the town; and there, oddly enough, I met with a man, a certain Captain Peterkin, who had been a friend of mine at college.'

'A visitor to Boulogne?' I inquired.

'Not exactly.'

'A resident?'

'Yes. The fact is, I lost sight of Peterkin when I left Oxford—and since that time he seems to have drifted into difficulties. We had a long talk. He is living here, he tells me, until his affairs are settled.'

I needed no further enlightenment—Captain Peterkin stood as plainly revealed to me as if I had known him for years. 'Isn't it a little imprudent,' I said, 'to renew your acquaintance with a man of that sort? Couldn't you have passed him, with a bow?'

Romayne smiled uneasily. 'I dare say you're right,' he answered, 'But, remember, I had left my aunt, feeling ashamed of the unjust way in which I had thought and spoken of her. How did I know that I mightn't be wronging an old friend next, if I kept Peterkin at a distance? His present position may be as much his misfortune, poor fellow, as his fault. I was half inclined to pass him, as you say—but I distrusted my own judgement. He held out his hand, and he was so glad to see me. It can't be helped now. I shall be anxious to hear your opinion of him.'

'Are we going to dine with Captain Peterkin?'

'Yes. I happened to mention that wretched dinner yesterday

at our hotel. He said, "Come to my boarding-house. Out of Paris, there isn't such a table d'hote in France." I tried to get off it not caring, as you know, to go among strangers—I said I had a friend with me. He invited you most cordially to accompany me. More excuses on my part only led to a painful result. I hurt Peterkin's feelings. "I'm down in the world," he said, "and I'm not fit company for you and your friends. I beg your pardon for taking the liberty of inviting you!" He turned away with tears in his eyes. What could I do?'

I thought to myself, 'You could have lent him five pounds, and got rid of his invitation without the slightest difficulty.' If I had returned in reasonable time to go out with Romayne, we might not have met the captain—or, if we had met him, my presence would have prevented the confidential talk and the invitation that followed. I felt I was to blame—and yet, how could I help it? It was useless to remonstrate: the mischief was done.

We left the Old Town on our right hand, and drove on, past a little colony of suburban villas, to a house standing by itself, surrounded by a stone wall. As we crossed the front garden on our way to the door, I noticed against the side of the house two kennels, inhabited by two large watch-dogs. Was the proprietor afraid of thieves?

III

The moment we were introduced to the drawing-room, my suspicions of the company we were likely to meet with were fully confirmed.

'Cards, billiards, and betting'—there was the inscription legibly written on the manner and appearance of Captain Peterkin. The bright-eyed yellow old lady who kept the boarding-house would have been worth five thousand pounds in jewellery alone, if the ornaments which profusely covered her had been genuine precious stones. The younger ladies present had their cheeks as highly rouged and their eyelids as elaborately pencilled in black as if they were going on the stage, instead of going to dinner. We found these fair creatures drinking Madeira as a whet to their appetites. Among the men, there were two who struck me as the most finished and complete blackguards whom I had ever met within all my experience, at home and abroad. One, with a brown face and a broken nose, was presented to us by the title of 'Commander', and was described as a person of great wealth and distinction in Peru, travelling for amusement. The other wore a military uniform and decorations, and was spoken of as 'the General.' A bold bullying manner, a fat sodden face, little leering eyes, and greasy-looking hands, made this man so repellent to me that I privately longed to kick him. Romayne had evidently been announced, before our arrival, as a landed gentleman with a large income. Men and women vied in servile attentions to him. When we went into the dining-room, the fascinating creature who sat next to him held her fan before her face, and so made a private interview of it between the rich Englishman and herself. With regard to the dinner, I shall only report that it justified Captain Peterkin's boast, in some degree at least. The wine was good, and the conversation became gay to the verge of indelicacy. Usually the most temperate of men, Romayne was tempted by his neighbours into drinking freely. I was unfortunately seated at the opposite extremity of the table, and I had no opportunity of warning him.

The dinner reached its conclusion, and we all returned together, on the foreign plan, to coffee and cigars in the drawing-room. The women smoked, and drank liqueurs as well as coffee, with the men. One of them went to the piano, and a little impromptu ball followed, the ladies dancing with their cigarettes in their mouths. Keeping my eyes and ears on the alert, I saw an innocent-looking table, with a surface of rosewood, suddenly develop a substance of green cloth. At the same time, a neat little roulette-table made its appearance from a hiding-place in a sofa. Passing near the venerable landlady, I heard her ask the servant, in a whisper, 'if the dogs were loose?' After what I had observed, l could only conclude that the dogs were used as a patrol, to give the alarm in case of a descent of the police. It was plainly high time to thank Captain Peterkin for his hospitality, and to take our leave.

'We have had enough of this,' I whispered to Romayne in English. 'Let us go.'

In these days it is a delusion to suppose that you can speak confidentially in the English language, when French people are within hearing. One of the ladies asked Romayne, tenderly, if he was tired of her already. Another reminded him that it was raining heavily (as we could all hear), and suggested waiting until it it cleared up. The hideous General waved his greasy hand in the direction of the card table, and said, 'The game is waiting for us.'

Romayne was excited, but not stupefied, by the wine he had drunk. He answered, discreetly enough, 'I must beg you to excuse me; I am a poor card player.'

The General suddenly looked gave. 'You are speaking, sir, under a strange misapprehension,' he said. 'Our game is lansquenet—essentially a game of chance. With luck, the poorest player is a match for the whole table.'

Romayne persisted in his refusal. As a matter of course, I supported him, with all needful care to avoid giving offence. The General took offence, nevertheless. He crossed his arms on his breast, and looked at us fiercely.

'Does this mean, gentlemen, that you distrust the company?' he asked.

The broken-nosed Commander, hearing the question, immediately joined us, in the interests of peace-bearing with him the elements of persuasion, under the form of a lady on his arm.

The lady stepped briskly forward, and tapped the General on the shoulder with her fan. 'I am one of the company,' she said, 'and I am sure Mr Romayne doesn't distrust *me*.' She turned to Romayne with her most irresistible smile. 'A gentleman always plays cards,' she resumed, 'when he has a lady for a partner. Let us join our interests at the table—and, dear Mr Romayne, don't risk too much!' She put her pretty little purse into his hand, and looked as if she had been in love with him for half her lifetime.

The fatal influence of the sex, assisted by wine, produced the inevitable result. Romayne allowed himself to be led to the card table. For a moment the General delayed the beginning of the game. After what had happened, it was necessary that he should assert the strict sense of justice that was in him. 'We are all honourable men,' he began.

'And brave men,' the Commander added, admiring the General.

'And brave men,' the General admitted, admiring the Commander. 'Gentlemen, if I have been led into expressing myself with unnecessary warmth of feeling, I apologize, and regret it.'

'Nobly spoken!' the Commander pronounced. The General put his hand on his heart and bowed. The game began.

As the poorest man of the two, I had escaped the attentions lavished by the ladies on Romayne. At the same time, I was obliged to pay for my dinner, by taking some part in the proceedings of the evening. Small stakes were allowed, I found, at roulette; and, besides, the heavy chances in favour of the table made it hardly worth while to run the risk of cheating in this case. I placed myself next to the least rascally-looking man in the company, and played roulette.

For a wonder, I was successful at the first attempt. My neighbour handed me my winnings. 'I have lost every farthing I possess,' he whispered to me, piteously, 'and I have a wife and children at home.' I lent the poor wretch five francs. He smiled faintly as he looked at the money. 'It reminds me,' he said, 'of my last transaction, when I borrowed of that gentleman there, who is betting on the General's luck at the card table. Beware of employing him as I did. What do you think I got for my note of hand of four thousand francs? A hundred bottles of champagne, fifty bottles of ink, fifty bottles of blacking, three dozen handkerchiefs, two pictures by unknown masters, two shawls, one hundred maps, *and*—five francs.'

'We went on playing. My luck deserted tile; I lost, and lost, and lost again. From time to time I looked round at the card table. The 'deal' had fallen early to the General, and it seemed to be indefinitely prolonged. A heap of notes and gold (won mainly from Romayne, as I afterwards discovered) lay before him. As for my neighbour, the unhappy possessor of the bottles of blacking, the pictures by unknown masters, and the rest of it, he won, and then rashly presumed on his good fortune. Deprived of his last farthing, he retired into a corner of the room, and consoled himself with a cigar. I had just risen, to follow his example, when a furious uproar burst out at the card table.

I saw Romayne spring up, and snatch the cards out of the General's hand. 'You scoundrel!' he shouted, 'you are cheating!' The General started to his feet in a fury. 'You lie!' he cried. I attempted to interfere, but Romayne had already seen the necessity of controlling himself. 'A gentleman doesn't accept an insult from a swindler,' he said coolly. 'Accept this, then!' the General answered—and spat on him. In an instant Romayne knocked him down.

The blow was dealt straight between his eyes: he was a gross big-boned man, and he fell heavily. For the time he was stunned. The women ran, screaming, out of the room. The peaceable Commander trembled from head to foot. Two of the men present, who, to give them their due, were no cowards, locked the doors. 'You don't go,' they said, 'till we see whether he recovers or not.' Cold water, assisted by the landlady's smelling salts, brought the General to his senses after a while. He whispered something to one of his friends, who immediately turned to me. 'The General challenges Mr Romayne,' he said. 'As one of his seconds, I demand an appointment for tomorrow morning.' I refused to make any appointment unless the doors were first unlocked, and we were left free to depart. 'Our carriage is waiting outside,' I added. 'If it returns to the hotel without us, there will be an inquiry.' This latter consideration had its effect. On their side, the doors were opened. On our side, the appointment was made. We left the house.

V

We were punctual to the appointed hour—eight o'clock.

The second who acted with me was a French gentleman, a relative of one of the officers who had brought the challenge. At his suggestion, we had chosen the pistol as our weapon. Romayne, like most Englishmen at the present time, knew nothing of the use of the sword. He was almost equally inexperienced with the pistol.

Our opponents were late. They kept us waiting for more than ten minutes. It was not pleasant weather to wait in. The day had dawned damp and drizzling. A thick white fog was slowly rolling in on us from the sea.

When they did appear, the General was not among them. A tall, well-dressed young man saluted Romayne with stern courtesy, and said to a stranger who accompanied him, 'Explain the circumstances.'

The stranger proved to be a surgeon. He entered at once on the necessary explanation. The General was too ill to appear. He had been attacked that morning by a fit—the consequence of the blow that he had received. Under these circumstances, his eldest son (Maurice) was now on the ground to fight the duel, on his father's behalf; attended by the General's seconds, and with the General's full approval.

We instantly refused to allow the duel to take place, Romayne loudly declaring that he had no quarrel with the General's son. Upon this, Maurice broke away from his seconds; drew off one of his gloves; and stepping close up to Romayne, struck him on the face with the glove. 'Have you no quarrel with me now?' the young Frenchman asked. 'Must I spit on you, as my father did?' His seconds dragged him away, and apologized to us for the outbreak. But the mischief was done. Romayne's fiery temper flashed in his eyes. 'Load the pistols,' he said. After the insult publicly offered to him, and the outrage publicly threatened, there was no other course to take.

It had been left to us to produce the pistols. We therefore requested the seconds of our opponent to examine, and to load them. While this was being done, the advancing sea-fog so completely enveloped us, that the duelists were unable to see each other. We were obliged to wait for the chance of a partial clearing in the atmosphere. Romayne's temper had become calm again. The generosity of his nature spoke in the words which he now addressed to his seconds.

'After all,' he said, 'the young man is a good son—he is

bent on redressing what he believes to be his father's wrong. Does his flipping his glove in my face matter to me? I think I shall fire in the air.'

'I shall refuse to act as your second if you do,' answered the French gentleman who was assisting us. 'The General's son is famous for his skill with the pistol. If you didn't see it in his face just now, I did—he means to kill you. Defend your life, sir!' I spoke quite as strongly, to the same purpose, when my turn came. Romayne yielded—he placed himself unreservedly in our hands.

In a quarter of an hour the fog lifted a little. We measured the distance, having previously arranged (at my suggestion) that the two men should both fire at the same moment, at a given signal. Romayne's composure, as they faced each other, was, in a man of his irritable nervous temperament, really wonderful. I placed him sideways, in a position which in some degree lessened his danger, by lessening the surface exposed to the bullet. My French colleague put the pistol into his hand, and gave him the last word of advice. 'Let your arm hang loosely down, with the barrel of the pistol pointing straight to the ground. When you hear the signal, only lift your arm as far as the elbow; keep the elbow pressed against your side—and fire.' We could do no more for him. As we drew aside—I own it—my tongue was like a cinder in my mouth, and a horrid inner cold crept through me to the marrow of my bones.

The signal was given, and the two shots were fired at the same time.

My first look was at Romayne. He took off his hat, and handed it to me with a smile. His adversary's bullet had cut a piece out of the brim of his hat, on the right side. He had literally escaped by a hairbreadth.

While I was congratulating him, the fog gathered again

more thickly than ever. Looking anxiously towards the ground occupied by our adversaries, we could only see vague, shadowy forms hurriedly crossing and re-crossing each other in the mist. Something had happened! My French colleague took my arm and pressed it significantly. 'Leave me to inquire,' he said. Romayne tried to follow; I held him back, neither of us exchanged a word.

The fog thickened and thickened, until nothing was to be seen. Once we heard the surgeon's voice, calling impatiently for a light to help him. No light appeared that we could see. Dreary as the fog itself, the silence gathered round us again. On a sudden broken, horribly broken, by another voice, strange to both it was one of us, shrieking hysterically through the impenetrable mist. 'Where is he?' the voice cried, in the French language. 'Assassin! Assassin! Where are you?' Was it a woman? or was it a boy? We heard nothing more. The effect upon Romayne was terrible to see. He who had calmly confronted the weapon lifted to kill him, shuddered dumbly like a terror-stricken animal. I put my arm round him, and hurried him away from the place.

We waited at the hotel until our French friend joined us. After a brief interval he appeared, announcing that the surgeon would follow him.

The duel had ended fatally. The chance course of the bullet, urged by Romayne's unpractised hand, had struck the General's son just above the right nostril—had penetrated to the back of his neck—and had communicated a fatal shock to the spinal marrow. He was a dead man before they could take him back to his father's house.

So far, our fears were confirmed. But there was something else to tell, for which our worst presentiments had not prepared us.

A younger brother of the fallen man (a boy of thirteen

years old) had secretly followed the duelling party, on their way from his father's house—had hidden himself—and had seen the dreadful end. The seconds only knew of it when he burst out of his place of concealment, and fell on his knees by his dying brother's side. His were the frightful cries which we had heard from invisible lips. The slayer of his brother was the 'assassin' whom he had vainly tried to discover through the fathomless obscurity of the mist.

We both looked at Romayne. He silently looked back at us, like a man turned to stone. I tried to reason with him.

'Your life was at your opponent's mercy,' I said. 'It was *he* who was skilled in the use of the pistol; your risk was infinitely greater than his. Are you responsible for an accident? Rouse yourself, Romayne! Think of the time to come, when all this will be forgotten.'

'Never,' he said, 'to the end of my life.'

He made that reply in dull monotonous tones. His eyes looked wearily and vacantly straight before him. I spoke to him again. He remained impenetrably silent; he appeared not to hear, or not to understand me. The surgeon came in, while I was still at a loss what to say or do next. Without waiting to be asked for his opinion, he observed Romayne attentively, and then drew me away into the next room.

'Your friend is suffering from a severe nervous shock,' he said. 'Can you tell me anything of his habits of life?'

I mentioned the prolonged night studies, and the excessive use of tea. The surgeon shook his head.

'If you want my advice,' he proceeded, 'take him home at once. Don't subject him to further excitement, when the result of the duel is known in the town. If it ends in our appearing in a court of law, it will be a mere formality in this case, and you can surrender when the time comes. Leave me your address in London.'

I felt that the wisest thing I could do was to follow his advice. The boat crossed to Folkestone at an early hour that day—we had no time to lose. Romayne offered no objection to our return to England; he seemed perfectly careless of what became of him. 'Leave me quiet,' he said: 'and do as you like.' I wrote a few lines to Lady Berrick's medical attendant, informing him of the circumstances. A quarter of an hour afterwards we were on board the steamboat.

THE CASK OF AMONTILLADO

Edgar Allan Poe

The thousand injuries of Fortunato I had borne as I best could, but when he ventured upon insult, I vowed revenge. You, who so well know the nature of my soul, will not suppose, however, that I gave utterance to a threat. *At length* I would be avenged; this was a point definitely settled—but the very definitiveness with which it was resolved, precluded the idea of risk. I must not only punish, but punish with impunity. A wrong is unredressed when retribution overtakes its redresser. It is equally unredressed when the avenger fails to make himself felt as such to him who has done the wrong.

It must be understood that neither by word nor deed had I given Fortunato cause to doubt my good will. I continued, as was my wont, to smile in his face, and he did not perceive that my smile *now* was at the thought of his immolation.

He had a weak point—this Fortunato—although in other regards he was a man to be respected and even feared. He prided himself on his connoisseurship in wine. Few Italians have the true virtuoso spirit. For the most part their enthusiasm is adopted to suit the time and opportunity—to practise imposture upon the British and Austrian *millionaires*. In painting and gemmary, Fortunato, like his countrymen, was a quack—but in the matter of old wines he was sincere. In this respect I did not differ from him materially: I was skilful in the Italian vintages myself, and bought largely whenever I could.

It was about dusk, one evening during the supreme madness of the carnival season, that I encountered my friend. He accosted me with excessive warmth, for he had been drinking much. The man wore motley. He had on a tight-fitting parti-striped dress, and his head was surmounted by the conical cap and bells. I was so pleased to see him, that I thought I should never have done wringing his hand.

I said to him—'My dear Fortunato, you are luckily met. How remarkably well you are looking today! But I have received a pipe of what passes for Amontillado, and I have my doubts.'

'How?' said he. 'Amontillado? A pipe? Impossible! And in the middle of the carnival!'

'I have my doubts,' I replied; 'and I was silly enough to pay the full Amontillado price without consulting you in the matter. You were not to be found, and I was fearful of losing a bargain.'

'Amontillado!'

'I have my doubts.'

'Amontillado!'

'And I must satisfy them.'

'Amontillado!'

'As you are engaged, I am on my way to Luchesi. If any one has a critical turn, it is he. He will tell me—'

'Luchesi cannot tell Amontillado from Sherry.'

'And yet some fools will have it that his taste is a match for your own.'

'Come, let us go.'

'Whither?'

'To your vaults.'

'My friend, no; I will not impose upon your good nature. I perceive you have an engagement. Luchesi—'

'I have no engagement;—come.'

'My friend, no. It is not the engagement, but the severe

cold with which I perceive you are afflicted. The vaults are insufferably damp. They are encrusted with nitre.'

'Let us go, nevertheless. The cold is merely nothing. Amontillado! You have been imposed upon. And as for Luchesi, he cannot distinguish Sherry from Amontillado.'

Thus speaking, Fortunato possessed himself of my arm. Putting on a mask of black silk, and drawing a *roquelaire* closely about my person, I suffered him to hurry me to my palazzo.

There were no attendants at home; they had absconded to make merry in honour of the time. I had told them that I should not return until the morning, and had given them explicit orders not to stir from the house. These orders were sufficient, I well knew, to insure their immediate disappearance, one and all, as soon as my back was turned.

I took from their sconces two flambeaux, and giving one to Fortunato, bowed him through several suites of rooms to the archway that led into the vaults. I passed down a long and winding staircase, requesting him to be cautious as he followed. We came at length to the foot of the descent, and stood together on the damp ground of the catacombs of the Montresors.

The gait of my friend was unsteady, and the bells upon his cap jingled as he strode.

'The pipe,' said he.

'It is farther on,' said I; 'but observe the white web-work which gleams from these cavern walls.'

He turned towards me, and looked into my eyes with two filmy orbs that distilled the rheum of intoxication.

'Nitre?' he asked, at length.

'Nitre,' I replied. 'How long have you had that cough?'

'Ugh! ugh! ugh!—ugh! ugh! ugh!—ugh! ugh! ugh!—ugh! ugh! ugh!—ugh! ugh! ugh!'

My poor friend found it impossible to reply for many

minutes.

'It is nothing,' he said, at last.

'Come,' I said, with decision, 'we will go back; your health is precious. You are rich, respected, admired, beloved; you are happy, as once I was. You are a man to be missed. For me it is no matter. We will go back; you will be ill, and I cannot be responsible. Besides, there is Luchesi—'

'Enough,' he said; 'the cough is a mere nothing; it will not kill me. I shall not die of a cough.'

'True—true,' I replied; 'and, indeed, I had no intention of alarming you unnecessarily—but you should use all proper caution. A draught of this Medoc will defend us from the damps.'

Here I knocked off the neck of a bottle which I drew from a long row of its fellows that lay upon the mould.

'Drink,' I said, presenting him the wine.

He raised it to his lips with a leer. He paused and nodded to me familiarly, while his bells jingled.

'I drink,' he said, 'to the buried that repose around us.'

'And I to your long life.'

He again took my arm, and we proceeded.

'These vaults,' he said, 'are extensive.'

'The Montresors,' I replied, 'were a great and numerous family.'

'I forget your arms.'

'A huge human foot d'or, in a field azure; the foot crushes a serpent rampant whose fangs are imbedded in the heel.'

'And the motto?'

'*Nemo me impune lacessit.*'

'Good!' he said.

The wine sparkled in his eyes and the bells jingled. My own fancy grew warm with the Medoc. We had passed through walls of piled bones, with casks and puncheons intermingling, into the inmost recesses of catacombs. I paused again, and this time I made bold to seize Fortunato by an arm above the elbow.

'The nitre!' I said; 'see, it increases. It hangs like moss upon the vaults. We are below the river's bed. The drops of moisture trickle among the bones. Come, we will go back ere it is too late. Your cough—'

'It is nothing,' he said; 'let us go on. But first, another draught of the Medoc.'

I broke and reached him a flagon of De Grave. He emptied it at a breath. His eyes flashed with a fierce light. He laughed and threw the bottle upwards with a gesticulation I did not understand.

I looked at him in surprise. He repeated the movement—a grotesque one.

'You do not comprehend?' he said.

'Not I,' I replied.

'Then you are not of the brotherhood.'

'How?'

'You are not of the masons.'

'Yes, yes,' I said; 'yes, yes.'

'You? Impossible! A mason?'

'A mason,' I replied.

'A sign,' he said, 'a sign'.

'It is this,' I answered, producing a trowel from beneath the folds of my *roquelaire*.

'You jest,' he exclaimed, recoiling a few paces. 'But let us proceed to the Amontillado.'

'Be it so,' I said, replacing the tool beneath the cloak and again offering him my arm. He leaned upon it heavily. We continued our route in search of the Amontillado. We passed through a range of low arches, descended, passed on, and descending again, arrived at a deep crypt, in which the foulness of the air caused our flambeaux rather to glow than flame.

At the most remote end of the crypt there appeared another less spacious one. Its walls had been lined with human remains, piled to the vault overhead, in the fashion of the great catacombs of Paris. Three sides of this interior crypt were still ornamented in this manner. From the fourth side the bones had been thrown down, and lay promiscuously upon the earth, forming at one point a mound of some size. Within the wall thus exposed by the displacing of the bones, we perceived a still interior recess, in depth about four feet, in width three, in height six or seven. It seemed to have been constructed for no especial use within itself, but formed merely the interval between two of the colossal supports of the roof of the catacombs, and was backed by one of their circumscribing walls of solid granite.

It was in vain that Fortunato, uplifting his dull torch, endeavoured to pry into the depth of the recess. Its termination the feeble light did not enable us to see.

'Proceed,' I said; 'herein is the Amontillado. As for Luchesi—'

'He is an ignoramus,' interrupted my friend, as he stepped unsteadily forward, while I followed immediately at his heels. In an instant he had reached the extremity of the niche, and finding his progress arrested by the rock, stood stupidly bewildered. A moment more and I had fettered him to the granite. In its surface were two iron staples, distant from each other about two feet, horizontally. From one of these depended a short chain, from the other a padlock. Throwing the links about his waist, it was but the work of a few seconds to secure it. He was too much astounded to resist. Withdrawing the key I stepped back from the recess.

'Pass your hand,' I said, 'over the wall; you cannot help feeling the nitre. Indeed, it is *very* damp. Once more let me *implore* you to return. No? Then I must positively leave you.

But I must first render you all the little attentions in my power.'

'The Amontillado!' ejaculated my friend, not yet recovered from his astonishment.

'True,' I replied; 'the Amontillado.'

As I said these words I busied myself among the pile of bones of which I have before spoken. Throwing them aside, I soon uncovered a quantity of building stone and mortar. With these materials and with the aid of my trowel, I began vigorously to wall up the entrance of the niche.

I had scarcely laid the first tier of the masonry when I discovered that the intoxication of Fortunato had in a great measure worn off. The earliest indication I had of this was a low moaning cry from the depth of the recess. It was *not* the cry of a drunken man. There was then a long and obstinate silence. I laid the second tier, and the third, and the fourth; and then I heard the furious vibrations of the chain. The noise lasted for several minutes, during which, that I might hearken to it with the more satisfaction, I ceased my labours and sat down upon the bones. When at last the clanking subsided, I resumed the trowel, and finished without interruption the fifth, the sixth, and the seventh tier. The wall was now nearly upon a level with my breast. I again paused, and holding the flambeaux over the mason-work, threw a few feeble rays upon the figure within.

A succession of loud and shrill screams, bursting suddenly from the throat of the chained form, seemed to thrust me violently back. For a brief moment I hesitated—I trembled. Unsheathing my rapier, I began to grope with it about the recess; but the thought of an instant reassured me. I placed my hand upon the solid fabric of the catacombs, and felt satisfied. I reapproached the wall; I replied to the yells of him who clamoured. I re-echoed—I aided—I surpassed them in volume and in strength. I did this, and the clamourer grew still.

It was now midnight, and my task was drawing to a close. I had completed the eighth, the ninth, and the tenth tier. I had finished a portion of the last and the eleventh; there remained but a single stone to be fitted and plastered in. I struggled with its weight; I placed it partially in its destined position. But now there came from out the niche a low laugh that erected the hair upon my head. It was succeeded by a sad voice, which I had difficulty in recognizing as that of the noble Fortunato. The voice said—

'Ha! ha! ha!—he! he! he!—a very good joke indeed—an excellent jest. We shall have many a rich laugh about it at the palazzo—he! he! he!—over our wine—he! he! he!'

'The Amontillado!' I said.

'He! he! he!—he! he! he!—yes, the Amontillado. But is it not getting late? Will not they be awaiting us at the palazzo, the Lady Fortunato and the rest? Let us be gone.'

'Yes,' I said, 'let us be gone.'

'For the love of God, Montresor!'

'Yes,' I said, 'for the love of God!'

But to these words I hearkened in vain for a reply. I grew impatient. I called aloud—

'Fortunato!'

No answer. I called again—

'Fortunato—'

No answer still. I thrust a torch through the remaining aperture and let it fall within. There came forth in reply only a jingling of the bells. My heart grew sick on account of the dampness of the catacombs. I hastened to make an end of my labour. I forced the last stone into its position; I plastered it up. Against the new masonry I re-erected the old rampart of bones. For the half of a century no mortal has disturbed them. *In pace requiescat!*